FIGHT TO THE DEATH!

Hobart felt the stink of blood and sweat gusting in his face as the huge mountain man bored in for the kill. Ruch's crazy yelling boomed in his head, and black specks jumped in front of his eyes. His fists hammered at the hairy, roaring face, but he couldn't break the giant's hold. It was like trying to fight a maddened grizzly with his bare hands. A blow like a hard-swung hammer threatened to cave in his ribs, and in a minute Ruch would start to kick him to pieces. Hardly able to see, Hobart's hand fumbled for the razor-edged skinning knife. He gripped it with the last of his strength and stabbed upward. Again and again, the big blade flashed in a killing arc.

We will send you a free catalog on request. Any titles not in your local book store can be purchased by mail. Send the price of the book plus 50¢ shipping charge to Belmont Tower Books, P.O. Box 270, Norwalk, Connecticut 06852.

Titles currently in print are available for industrial and sales promotion at reduced rates. Address inquiries to Tower Publications, Inc., Two Park Avenue, New York, New York 10016, Attention: Premium Sales Department.

THE WOLFER

James B. Chaffin

BELMONT TOWER BOOKS • NEW YORK CITY

A BELMONT TOWER BOOK

Published by

Tower Publications, Inc.
Two Park Avenue
New York, N.Y. 10016

Chapter
ONE

The calendar was a liar when it said spring was here. But in this high north country the calendar and nature rarely agreed. A cutting wind blew in from the river, and Gary Hobart shivered. He knew this jacket wasn't heavy enough when he started out, but his sheepskin was too disreputable to wear to a dance. It was greasy and black with wear, and Elizabeth would have taken one look at it and gasped in horror. But it had a tremendous advantage over this light jacket; it was warm.

He stepped down from the saddle and led Bullet into the runway of the livery stable. Old Priam came out of the heated cubicle he called his office. Gary got a glimpse of the glowing pot-bellied stove before Priam shut the door on it. He would almost prefer to spend the evening sitting beside Priam before that stove.

Priam frowned at the snow on Gary's boots. "Goddamned weather. Who'd think it'd snow this late in the year?"

"Anybody with any memory, Priam. April isn't over yet." And snow in Montana in May wasn't such a rarity that it would make a conversation piece. But he agreed with Priam's mood. A snow this late hurt everybody. A man was weary of a long, trying winter, and his bones ached for a glimpse of true spring. This snow fell yesterday, and four inches of it lay on the ground. It could easily be gone tomorrow night, if the soft, warm Chinook winds hit in the morning, but right now, a man felt he was in the heart of winter again.

Priam glared at him. "I've got a memory." He was muffled to the eyes, and the heavy scarf smothered his voice. "I just keep trying to kid myself that every snow is the last one."

Priam was old. He had few teeth left, and his face was seamed and sagging. Gary imagined that his blood must be thinning. These winters must be hell on the old.

"I've got a bottle in my saddlebag, Priam."

Priam brightened. "And I'll take it. Maybe it'll get me through this damned night. I'll even share it with you."

Gary was tempted, but if Elizabeth caught it on his breath, he knew how displeased she would be. He sighed and let the pleasant thought of the warming liquor go. "Guess not, Priam."

Priam was still indignant about the weather. "The damned Army had to pick tonight to have its ball. All evening I've been running in and out from the heat to the cold, to get somebody a horse, the next a buggy. Everybody in town wants something. I put on clothes and take them off. Best way in the world to catch a cold."

Gary knew an instant alarm. "You saved me a buggy, didn't you?"

"I wouldn't have, if you hadn't brought me the bottle."

Gary grinned. "It's not that big a bottle." Gary was fond of this old man. Priam was rough and caustic. In many ways he had the temperament of an Indian. Get on the wrong side of him, and he wouldn't pour water on you if you were on fire. But if he liked you, there wasn't anything he wouldn't do for you.

Priam lightly touched his arm. "I knew you wouldn't let me down. How'd the cattle winter, Gary?"

"Good." Gary's tone was absent. His mind wasn't on the cattle, one of the few times during a day when it happened. But he had gone through the winter well. He had gotten a figure just this week, and he had suffered less than five percent winter kill. Any rancher would tell you that was damned lucky or excellent management. He was proud of his ranch. It wasn't big by Montana standards. A dozen nearby ranches could have gulped him up without a labored breath; or so they had thought. A couple had tried it. They wouldn't try again.

He was making progress; it showed every year. But this was the year he wanted. If the spring calf crop was good, and the fall roundup and shipment brought in the money he thought it would, he had something he wanted to ask Elizabeth. God knew, he had put it off long enough. But a man wanted to have things as good as he could when he asked a woman to share them.

Priam gave him one more chance. "Sure you won't join me?" He turned and ambled away from Gary's shaking head.

Gary's eyes roamed over the part of Fort Benton he could see from the mouth of the runway. The town was growing every year. Pretty soon it was going to become so civilized around here that a man would feel the pinch of it hemming him in. He grinned at the absurdity. It would be a long time before Montana was settled to that degree.

The town had grown amazingly since the Army had set up a post here. The Army raised Fort Benton from

7

the status of a trading post to that of a thriving town. The Army spent a lot of money here, but only the townspeople were pleased, and some of those only within earshot of the military. An awful lot of people hated the troopers. Earned, Gary thought decisively. They were arrogant men, believing the uniform permitted them any excess. And they weren't doing a hell of a lot of good here any more.

Most of the Indian trouble was over. The post was supposed to protect the cattlemen from the raids of the reservation Indians. Gary's jaw hardened. He got mad every time he thought about it. All the Army did was protect the Indians. Gary didn't know of a single case where the Army brought back a rancher's stolen cattle. Maybe it just worked out that way, and maybe it wasn't accidental. Maybe it was part of a deliberate plan. It sure should keep down the cost of feeding those Indians.

He hadn't better voice any of these opinions to Elizabeth. She favored the presence of the military. The last time he had criticized the Army she had exploded in his face. He shouldn't bring anything up that would dim an evening of pleasure. But it was hard for a man to forget about something that rode him at all other times.

He looked at the snow-covered street with distaste. When it melted, it would be a morass of mud. The mournful blast of a steamboat whistle came from the direction of the wharves. He would bet that the pilot was certainly relieved at finally arriving in town. Running the Missouri River after dark was no playtime, especially when it was filled with floating ice. Something must have delayed the boat to arrive this late. The pilot's problem, he thought. Not mine.

Gary wasn't a tall man, but he was compactly built with most of his weight concentrated in his torso. He had the chest and shoulders of a man of much bigger frame, and there wasn't an ounce of waste meat on him. The weather and hardships had honed him fine. It had also given him an assurance. What a man did before, he could do again. He was orphaned at sixteen, and he had hung onto the ranch. He could take pride in that. It was tough country, and it took a man to carve out his niche.

He turned his head and stared down the dark length of the runway. What was taking Priam so long? He smiled ruefully. His one big fault was impatience. His face was sober, almost foreboding in repose, but a smile could lighten and liven it. His black hair closely fitted his skull. It was a good thing he had remembered to have it cut this week.

A heavy freighter slipped and lurched through the street, and he turned his attention to it. Fort Benton had every attribute to make itself grow. It was an important terminus for the river shipping. Its fur trade and traffic with the gold camps were diminishing, but enough new activities were building so that these losses were scarcely noticed. Ranching alone was becoming an important business. It was a wild town, and visitors were warned, "Walk in the middle of the street and mind your own business." The advice contained little jest.

Its streets were usually crowded. The new wooden walks were an improvement, and a man could pick out the saloons by the discarded playing cards on the walk before them. The fur trappers had thinned out, and in their place were the wolfers. They lived by killing and skinning wolves, and no tougher breed of man walked. They led a lonely, dangerous life and were disliked by everybody. Even in town they stayed with their own, and their sole purpose here seemed to be to see how drunk they could get. Nobody tried to upset the arrangement, for the wolfers were a surly lot with hair-trigger tempers. Fort Benton got them all, the wolfers, the illicit whiskey traders, the horse thieves and outlaws. Gary smiled. And a moment ago, he had been complaining because this country was getting too civilized.

He glanced again down the runway. He made allowances for an old man's slowness, but Priam seemed to be taking forever. He wished this damned night was over. He looked forward to an ordinary dance, but this was an Army ball, held at the post. Once a year the Army magnanimously included the prominent townspeople, and Elizabeth's father had received an invitation. Gary wasn't fooling himself. He was only going because he was Elizabeth's escort. He would spend most of the evening burning at the officers and their pretty dress uniforms. Most of them would have no partners of their own, and Gary knew how the evening would go. They would come up, click their heels and bow, and ask if they could have the pleasure of the lady's company for the next dance. It would happen where Elizabeth was concerned too often, particularly if Captain John Blakely was there. Gary hoped the bastard would be out on patrol somewhere.

He heard the rattle of wheels, and Priam came up, leading a bay horse hitched to a buggy.

"What were you doing, building it?"

Priam gave him an indignant look. "Wish now I hadn't taken time to clean it out."

Gary dropped his hand on the old man's shoulder. "Priam, I've got a big mouth."

"You sure as hell have. I hope Blakely gives you fits tonight."

Gary's eyes hardened. If the old man knew it, it must be all over town that Blakely was interested in Elizabeth

Danfield. He climbed into the buggy and looked down at Priam. "He won't!"

Priam cackled in wicked glee. Gary had let too much anger show in his tone.

Gary scowled at him. "I hope you get drunk enough to fall and bust your head open."

This only sent Priam into more convulsive laughter. Gary snapped the reins against the bay's rump and drove out onto the street. He would have to guard his feelings better, but Blakely was a burr under his saddle blanket. Something struck him, and he swore softly. Blakely had been assigned here two months ago, and Elizabeth seemed to have changed since then. His swearing strengthened. What a damned fool way to be thinking. He should have kicked Priam's ass for bringing up Blakely's name.

He drove the four blocks to the Danfield house. The distance to the post from here wasn't far, but a man couldn't expect his girl to walk it; particularly on a night like this.

The house was one of the better ones in town. It showed how well Sam Danfield was doing with his freighting business. If he knew Sam, Sam wasn't any happier than he was about this evening. But Danfield was almost forced to go because of the amount of business he got from the post. He sighed and climbed down. It was always the women who dragged men to affairs like his.

He trudged through the snow to the door and knocked.

Danfield opened the door and glared sourly at Gary. "Are you any happier about this than I am?"

Gary laughed. "Depends upon how happy you are, Sam."

"Damned little. Fasten this collar for me, will you?

11

I've been trying to get Abigail to do it for the last half-hour. But she's been too busy with her own dressing. I hate these damned collars!"

' He tilted his head back, and Gary tried to pull the two ends of the collar together. Danfield was a big man with a thickness through the neck. He had picked up weight around the belly, too. Gary could remember not too far back when Danfield had been as lean as a rawhide thong. But that had been when he was scrambling for business. A bank account wasn't the only thing prosperity built up.

He made a couple of futile attempts, and the collar slipped away just when he thought he had it.

"Gary, why do these fool affairs mean so much to a woman?"

Gary swore. "Will you quit talking? You made me lose it. I don't know, Sam. Maybe it's because they get to show off new clothes."

Danfield groaned. "When I think of what these two spent on this evening."

"Goddamn it, Sam. There it went again. You've got to get one of two things."

"What's that?" A suspicious look was in Danfield's eyes.

"A smaller neck or a bigger collar."

"That's damned funny. You've got to get it fastened. Try it once more."

The collar cut cruelly into Danfield's neck as Gary exerted merciless pressure. The collar button slipped into place, and Danfield's face turned an interesting shade of purple.

"My God," he wheezed. "I can't stand this all evening."

Gary reached out to remove it, and Danfield covered the button with both hands. His voice sounded strangled.

12

"I'll go as far as I can. Abigail will kill me, if I don't wear it." His eyes brightened. "Maybe I can step on her foot hard enough to make her want to come home early."

Gary's laughter broke off, as Elizabeth stepped into the room. She was a vision in a new green dress of some kind of shimmering material, though he thought it was cut too low in front. It showed a lot of her.

She waited for his approval, and though he didn't say a word she was satisfied with what showed in his face. The gown complimented her complexion. She had red hair and green eyes, and every time he saw her, he got hit in the stomach like this. He forgot all about Danfield's suffering, he forgot everything but her.

He started to move to her, then stopped. She was frowning, and he followed her eyes. His boots were snow- and mud-stained. He couldn't help it. They were polished before he left home. The ground hadn't been frozen when that snow fell, and underneath it was mud.

"He won't be the only one there with muddy boots," Danfield grunted. He weighed his daughter with speculative eyes and held whatever else was on his mind.

"I'll rub them off before we go in," Gary promised.

That satisfied her, for she moved to him and took his arm. "Gary, I'm so excited."

Her sparkling eyes told him that. This was a big night for her. Maybe some of her excitement would rub off on him.

Danfield tried to ease a finger between neck and collar. "Go ahead. If I know Abigail, it'll be another half-hour before we leave."

As Gary closed the door behind him, he heard Danfield say, "Oh, my God." He must be prying at that collar again.

13

Chapter
TWO

Elizabeth looked with dismay at the snow between her and the buggy. "I'll have to go back and get my overshoes."

Gary knew she didn't want to wear the heavy, ugly things over her dance shoes. "Why?" He swooped her into his arms before she realized what he was doing. She was a full-bodied woman, having more weight than he would have guessed. The pressure of her against him was a wonderfully exhilarating feeling. "I planned it this way."

She smiled back at him, and she was the girl he first knew, her eyes alert and interested. "And at the dance?"

"I imagine we can manage the same way."

She laughed and laid her cheek briefly against his. "Oh Gary, it's going to be a perfect evening."

A rush of feeling overwhelmed him. Nothing was changed between them. The fault was his. He had found flaws where none existed. This dance meant a great deal to her, and he must be careful not to spoil it in any way.

Her weight made the footing treacherous, and he took small, careful steps. He deposited her in the buggy, and he wasn't breathing too hard.

He drove to the Fort's stockade, and the wide double gates were open. The flames of pine-knot torches, on each side of the gate, jumped and danced in the breeze, throwing ever-changing patterns of light on the snow. He frowned at the parked vehicles outside the stockade, wondering why everybody had stopped her. Probably the first arrivals were timorous souls, and feeling the uneasy respect most people knew on Army property, had pulled up here. Other arrivals had merely followed suit. Well, he wasn't.

He started to drive on through, and a sentry stepped out in front of the horse. He hauled on the reins and swore under his breath. He had caught the man's movement early, or he might have run him down.

"Which building is the dance in, soldier?"

The soldier pointed. "There, sir." He was lanky and raw-boned, and his uniform fitted him poorly. A deep sullenness was stamped into his face, and the lower, pendant lip emphasized it. The twang in his voice was straight Missouri.

Gary could have picked out the right building by the light streaming from it. It lay better than a hundred yards across the compound.

Apologetically, the soldier cleared his throat. "But you can't drive in."

"Why not?"

"Colonel's orders, sir, when the ground is soft. He doesn't like to have the compound rutted."

Gary caught the sound of dismay Elizabeth made. She realized it, too. He couldn't carry her that far.

He managed to keep his temper. Another of the petty regulations the Army seemed to revel in. He wondered if this was an Army regulation or one of the Colonel's whims. It seemed the higher the rank, the greater the indulgement of personal whims. Didn't the Colonel realize he had invited guests here tonight?

15

"I'll just drive in, leave the lady, and come right back."

The soldier's face was still apologetic, but his head shake was determined. "I can't let you, sir."

"What can't you let him do, Mahoney?"

Mahoney whirled and came to smart attention. "Captain Blakely, sir. I didn't hear you."

"Were you awake, Mahoney? I'd be surprised if you were."

The light was sufficient for Gary to catch the savage glint in Mahoney's eyes. These two had had run-ins before.

"Captain." It galled Gary to keep his tone civil. Everything about this man rubbed him the wrong way. "The soldier says we can't drive across the compound."

Blakely stepped to the buggy. He was better than six feet tall, and he moved like a hungry cat. He had a tremendous span of shoulder, and his uniform fitted him perfectly. He was a handsome devil, but his eyes were mean, and he had a strutting arrogance that fitted that meanness. But women were attracted to him. Gary had noticed the lingering glances women put on him as he passed down the street in Benton. And he cut a wide swath with the dance-hall girls.

"Mahoney's right for once. Colonel's orders." He peered into the buggy, seeing Elizabeth for the first time. "Elizabeth! I didn't know it was you."

Her laugh was gay and bubbly. "John, I'm going to ruin my shoes."

Gary set his teeth. Where had they picked up a first name basis?

Blakely had a rich, infectious chuckle. "Now we can't have that, can we?"

Gary noticed he wore that damned dagger revolver in its special holster. Atken, the gunsmith in town, told him it was made in Paris by Le Faucheux sometime around 1858. It used percussion caps like the early Colts, and its wide blade extended better than six inches beyond its short barrel. It could stab or shoot, and Blakely had used the blade a short month ago. An Army court martial had tried him and found he had acted in self-defense. Nobody had any doubt it would come out that way. Some people muttered that Blakely had provoked the fight. Gary didn't know about that. He did know he didn't like the weapon, for he hated a damned knife man. He doubted it was regulation to carry it, but Blakely was an officer, and he bent regulations to his will.

Blakely had a foot on the buggy step. "Move over, Hobart. I'll drive you to the door. You can bring the buggy back."

Mahoney's face showed alarm. "But, sir—"

Blakely whirled on him. "Are you arguing with me?"

"No, sir. But the Colonel will blame me."

Blakely kept walking toward him. "You are arguing, Mahoney. I've never been able to teach you—" His face was close to Mahoney's, and he caught a whiff of his breath. "You've been drinking, Mahoney."

Mahoney's eyes were agonized. "No, sir." He reconsidered that. "Just one little one, Captain. It's a chilly night—"

"And you know what regulations say about drinking on duty. Report for the stable detail in the morning."

"But, Captain. I just came off it yesterday."

Blakely's face held evident pleasure. "You never learn, do you, Mahoney? This time, I'm going to forget you're on that detail."

He turned and climbed into the buggy. Gary glanced at Mahoney. That was about as much hating as he had ever seen in a face.

With Blakely there, the buggy's seat was a tight squeeze. The butt of that gun gouged into Gary's hip.

Blakely picked up the reins. "Hobart, you're lucky you don't have to handle the riffraff I do. But I'll break him."

Gary stared straight ahead. Blakely's chief interest was not in making a soldier; it was in breaking a man.

Blakely looked across him to Elizabeth. "Elizabeth, I go off duty shortly. Save me a dance."

Her laughter had a queer, excited note. "You know I will."

Blakely's laugh was low and assured. Two different kinds of laughter, but both of them had claws that raked Gary.

Blakely pulled up before the building. He jumped out before Gary could move. He ran around the buggy and held out his arms to Elizabeth.

"Don't you drop me," she warned.

Blakely picked her out of the buggy. "I wouldn't dare."

Gary sat there in burning silence.

Blakely turned his head over his shoulder. "Take it out of here, Hobart."

Gary swore all the way back to the gates. Blakely had outmaneuvered him every step of the way. He discounted the advantage of Blakely being on home grounds. He transferred some of his resentment to Elizabeth. She hadn't made it any harder for Blakely. He went back over it. What could he have done to change it? He could have refused to let Blakely drive the buggy onto the post. Then Elizabeth would have been furious at him for ruining her shoes. This had been one of those spots that he couldn't win whichever way he turned.

He tied the horse outside the stockade and came back through the gates. Mahoney glowered at him, and upon

18

impulse Gary stopped. "Sorry I got you in trouble, Mahoney."

It was the key that unlocked the door to invective Mahoney had been holding too long. "The rotten son-of-a-bitch. He looks for any little thing to hang me with. He's been on me ever since I got here. I get the stables again. Sergeant Catron will work my ass off to win more favor with Blakely. I'll get both of the bastards one of these days. I'll—" He realized he was talking to a civilian and abruptly shut his mouth. He had one more thing to say before he turned away. "If you done like I told you to at first, none of it would've happened." His final look said he gave Gary equal blame.

It probably wouldn't have happened, Gary admitted. That buggy, parked in the gate, had caught Blakely's attention and pulled him over. Mahoney had some justifaction to his feeling against him.

He plowed through the snow toward the lighted building. This evening was getting off to a hell of a fine start.

He stepped inside and looked around for Elizabeth. He wouldn't have been surprised to find Blakely with her, but she was alone. The building was a long hall of some kind, probably a mess hall. If so, the tables had been carried out, but the benches were lined up against the walls. Three enlisted men sat behind their instruments, a piano, a guitar and a violin. Their boots were polished, their hair plastered down, their uniforms spotless. They had the uneasy, self-conscious look of enlisted men wherever so much rank gathered. They were fooling around now to keep their hands occupied, playing a snatch of a tune, then jumping to another. Evidently, the Colonel wasn't here, and the dance couldn't start until he arrived.

Gary left muddy tracks across the floor, and Elizabeth frowned at them.

"There wasn't anything outside to wipe my boots on." That was perilously close to a snarl, and he changed his tone. "I couldn't use my handkerchief, could I?"

She gave him a slight, forgiving smile and looked toward the stir at the door. The Colonel had arrived, followed by his staff. He paraded down the middle of the hall, nodding and smiling. Colonel Stenton was a tall, gray-haired man with a ramrod bearing. Gary had no opinions one way or the other about him. He had had no dealings with the man.

Stenton raised his arm, and the music started. Gary held out his arms, and Elizabeth slipped into them. The music was surprisingly good, and they danced well together. All the earlier rancor vanished.

They caught a lot of eyes as they moved around the floor, and Gary suspected Elizabeth was the reason. She was a picture with her head thrown back and color glowing in her cheeks. He would ask nothing more than to keep the rest of the evening this way.

He got two straight dances with her before a brash Second Lieutenant came over and asked permission for the next one. She looked questioningly at Gary, and he nodded. What else could he do?

His face was morose as he watched them. The Lieutenant talked a mile a minute, and Elizabeth listened attentively. She had that knack of making a man feel important. Gary wished he was talking to her.

The Lieutenant's audacity emboldened some of the other officers, and they were at Elizabeth's side when the Lieutenant brought her back.

"No!" Gary's voice was decisive. "This next one is mine."

She stepped out onto the floor with him, wearing a mocking smile. "How flattering."

His arms tightened about her. "You know it's more than that."

"I know," she murmured, and all his sourness faded. This evening was a fine, shining thing.

The mood faded before the music stopped. He saw Blakely come into the building, and that edge of temper scraped at him again. Blakely stopped just inside the door. His head turned first one way, then the other, and he seemed to be looking for somebody. Gary doubted that. Blakely wanted to be seen. He made quite a picture. The uniform was new, probably saved for just such an occasion, and a man could see his face in his boots. His face shone from a recent washing, and his blonde hair lay smoothly along his head.

Gary turned Elizabeth before she saw him. That would happen soon enough. He wished there was some place he could take her.

Blakely was there the moment Gary brought her to the side of the hall. He bowed low over her hand, and Gary had an insane impulse to hit the back of that blonde head.

Blakely raised his head. He had good teeth, and he displayed them. "Elizabeth, I must take you over to meet the Colonel."

Gary couldn't believe it, but Elizabeth looked flustered. He wouldn't have believed that rank was that important to her.

She took Blakely's arm without asking Gary's consent. He realized his teeth were aching, as he watched them cross the floor, and he forced his jaws to ease up.

He joined Danfield and Abigail, and both of them looked unhappy.

"Abigail got her feet wet." Danfield stretched his neck as though he hoped that would ease the pressure. "I told her to wear her overshoes. She blames me because I didn't make her." He turned his head, following the dancers. "Say, Elizabeth's dancing with the Colonel."

"Blakely introduced her."

"Good for business." Danfield nudged his wife. "Mother, do you see that?"

I'll be damned, Gary thought. That eagle on Stenton's shoulder means something to him, too. He lessened the harshness of the indictment. Danfield got a lot of freighting from Stenton.

Abigail shrugged. Her feet were more important right now. Her shoes were too light to stand much wading in the snow, and her feet were probably soaked. "Sam, I don't want to stay here very long."

"Aw now I'm sorry." But Danfield winked at Gary.

Danfield was going to get out of his misery fairly soon. Gary wondered how long his would last.

Blakely didn't bring Elizabeth back after the dance. He kept her near the Colonel, and Gary wanted to go over and get her. He wasn't that reckless. He knew how that would sit with her.

Blakely claimed the next dance, and Gary's eyes smoldered. He was going to have to stop that smart bastard in his tracks.

He intercepted them when they came off the floor and took hold of her arm. "My dance, Elizabeth."

Her face was stricken. "Oh Gary, I'd forgotten. I promised it to John."

His eyes were stubborn. "Then unpromise it." His hold was slipping on his temper, and he didn't care too much.

Her eyes were smokey as she looked at him, and he

22

thought the rebellion in them would flare into open refusal.

Blakely laughed easily. But only with his lips. A wicked spark burned in his eyes. "I give you your promise back, Elizabeth. I wouldn't want to be the one who spoiled your evening."

Elizabeth gave him a grateful smile. Gary boiled inwardly. He was in the wrong again.

Blakely checked them before they went out onto the floor. "But I should have the one after this to make up for my loss."

He pulled out that richly embossed, gold-cased watch. Gary had seen it before. Blakely had to be proud of that watch to display it so often. It had probably cost more than Gary had earned in some of the bad years.

Blakely sighed and put the watch away. "I hope I can last a few more minutes."

Elizabeth's smile at him broke the thin leash on Gary's temper. "You'll wait a hell of a lot longer than that. I brought her, and I'm going to dance with her." He heard her gasp, but his attention was centered on that wicked flame. It filled Blakely's eyes now.

"Gary!" Elizabeth was furious. "People are staring at us."

His and Blakely's attitude was tension-filled. Even if people couldn't hear a word, they could guess.

The music started, and Elizabeth tugged on his arm. She didn't speak until they were on the floor. "That was disgraceful. He was only being kind."

"Kind, hell. If he comes near you again, I'm going to knock his head off."

He had never seen that white line around her lips before. She struggled to get the words out. "Take me home."

23

He almost gave way to weakness and begged. He looked at that cold, set face. Begging wouldn't do any good. "If that's the way you want it."

He got her cloak, and she wouldn't let him help her on with it. He stalked out of the hall after her. It was all right with him.

She wouldn't let him go after the buggy, either. She walked ahead, and he followed her across the compound. His anger was fading. He had handled that like a love-sick schoolboy. She had a right to some of her anger.

She struck at his hand when he tried to help her into the buggy. The embers of his anger weren't all dead. It was easy to fan them back into life. "All right. I ruined your evening. What about mine? Him hanging around every minute—"

Her look seared him. "I don't know if I'll ever forgive you."

He better hadn't say any more. It was bad enough already. They didn't exchange a word all the way home.

Chapter
THREE

She made no show of asking him in. In fact, she shut the door on his plaintive, "Elizabeth." He stayed on the porch for several minutes, hoping she might relent and open the door.

He saw how groundless his hopes were. All right, and maybe he wouldn't come back for a long time. He went back over the evening. He saw where he might have smoothed his behavior a little but there was nothing that he would basically change. If it had offended her this much, he didn't give a damn. The hollow in his stomach called him a liar.

He didn't see the figure until he almost reached the buggy. It stepped away from its shadow, and Gary's start of alarm subsided. What the hell was Blakely doing here?

"We're going to finish our talk, Hobart."

Gary's jaw jutted. "I've got nothing to say to you."

Blakely blocked his way to the buggy. "I say you have."

The moon was out, and Gary's eyes swept over him. He saw the pleased shine in Blakely's eyes and understood. In Blakely's head, he had raked his pride, and Blakely wanted compensation. He couldn't get out of the kind of talk Blakely had in mind. He also saw something else. Blakely was wearing the dagger gun.

Gary held his hands out from his sides. "I'm not armed."

"Not that kind of talk, Hobart. I'm going to give you something you'll remember for a long time." He unbuckled the gun belt and turned back to the buggy. He draped it across a wheel and started unfastening the buttons of his tunic. "You can get out of it by running."

Gary had no thought of running. He welcomed this. But he threw an uneasy glance toward the house. If Elizabeth saw this, she'd blame him for it, too.

He removed his jacket, and the chill night air cut through his shirt. That wouldn't last long. He would be heated up soon enough.

They stood, sizing each other up. Then Blakely started a slow circling. Gary moved with him. He knew nothing about the man's ability except that Blakely had the reputation of a brawler. He had size and reach, but Gary was too mad to consider those advantages.

He sprang in and threw a left hand at Blakely's face. Blakely moved well. He almost got his face out of the way. But Gary's knuckles caught him along the cheekbone and slid along it.

Blakely blinked and shook his head. The spreading bruise showed black in the moonlight. His "ah" sounded pleased.

He came in hard, throwing a long, looping blow at the end of his rush. Gary saw it coming in time to get a shoulder between it and his jaw.

Blakely still sounded pleased. "You're going to make this worth my time, Hobart."

The little anxious tension left Gary. A man never knew how he was going to do when he was up against another for the first time, but he could handle Blakely. He felt it.

26

"Without your bars, Blakely, you're nothing but mouth."

Blakely's eyes turned wild. "You're running up a big bill, Hobart. And I'll collect every damned bit of it."

He leaped at Gary, and Gary met it. He got a stinging blow in through Blakely's hands, and it landed on his nose. He drew one on his forehead that put a ringing in his head and buried the other hand in Blakely's belly. They closed and half wrestled, half punched, the blows smothered and ineffectual. He threw Blakely from him and discovered something else that was important. He was the stronger.

He shook his head to clear the ringing. He wasn't chilly now. Blakely's nose bled, and the flow looked black in the moonlight. He rubbed the back of his hand across it and looked at the smear of blood on it. A maniacal rage twisted his face, and he jumped at Gary with animal fury replacing skill and finesse. The rush blocked any thought of offense, and Gary covered and backed before it. Maybe he was a little premature in thinking he was the stronger. Blakely threw a storm of punches most of them landing on Gary's arms and the top of his head. But a couple of them got through, and he felt their jolting impact.

Blakely's breathing was a sobbing tear in his throat, and he expended energy recklessly. If Gary could ride this out, it was working for him, for it should leave Blakely leg and arm weary. The treacherous snow betrayed him. And one of those half smothered blows helped it along. The blow glanced off of Gary's chin just as he tried to back and cut, and his feet went out from under him. He landed on his back and heard Blakely's hoarse grunt of triumph. Blakely dove at him, and Gary's attempted rolling wasn't in time. Blakely landed on him,

27

and his fists opened and became claws, tearing at Gary's face. Gary had to protect his face, and at the same time try to throw Blakely off of him. He rolled first one way, then the other, and Blakely threw his weight to meet and block the roll. That superior weight was beginning to tell, and Gary was taking a savage mauling.

He sensed the knee lifting and slamming at his crotch. He twisted his body, and most of the knee's force missed the target it wanted. But it was enough to send waves of sickness through him. If the knee had been an inch truer, he would have been crippled. The nausea put a sour gagging in his throat, and he wanted so much to quit this struggling and let the hovering blackness take him. He could lose it all in this moment of weakness. He reached deep inside him, and there was enough determination left to answer his question.

He got an arm free, but any blow he could throw would be weak. Instead, he jabbed his elbow into Blakely's Adam's apple, and the shorter, straighter blow made it a brutal thing.

Blakely reared up and clutched at his throat. The gargled, choking sounds sounded like an animal in distress. Gary shoved at him with both hands and toppled him sideways. Blakely's legs were partially across him, and he crawled free of their entangling weight.

He didn't make it on his first attempt to stand. It took tremendous effort to get his feet under him, and he stood on wobbly legs, gulping in air.

Blakely still writhed in the snow, and as Gary looked at him, he knew some of that senseless rage that had possessed Blakely. He knew one thing for certain. He wasn't going to let the bastard get up.

Blakely was lifting his head, as Gary reached him. He kicked at the rising face, and his timing and strength

28

were both shot. He intended to drive the boot full into the face, and instead the edge of the sole scraped along Blakely's jaw.

But it was enough to put Blakely back into the snow, and his eyes were blank and uncorrelated.

He dropped with both knees on Blakely's chest, and the impact exploded the air from Blakely's lungs. He slugged at him with both hands, and the blows gained strength. He didn't know how long he flailed away, but he could scarcely lift his hand for another blow. He realized the head was rocking back and forth with no resistance in it. He was hitting an unconscious man. He looked at the bloody, ruined face and knew a wicked satisfaction.

He pushed himself off the inanimate form, and it was an effort to stand. My God, he was weak. He could feel the stinging of a thousand cuts as the night air bit into them. All he wanted to do was to lie down. He had better get that buggy back to Priam before he fell on his face.

He wobbled toward it, dully swearing at the slippery footing and his weakness. He threw out a hand to catch a buggy wheel for support and misjudged his distance. The motion pulled him forward, and he fell into the steel-rimmed wheel. He struck his forehead against it, and a million red lights burst before his eyes. They were followed immediately by a heavy, black curtain that blotted out everything.

Mahoney staggered down the street. He had only intended upon drinking enough whiskey to warm him, but he had taken it too fast and so overestimated the amount he could handle. It was hitting him hard and making his legs limber. He had to get back to the post before anybody discovered his absence. Larson had promised to cover for him, and nobody would be aware of the exchange while the dance was going on. He argued with himself, as he lurched along. With what was ahead of him tomorrow, wasn't he entitled to a few minutes? Damned right, he was.

Vaguely, he looked about him. He didn't recognize this street at all. Damned if he hadn't taken a wrong turn somewhere back there.

He saw the buggy ahead and peered at it. A wave of self-pity engulfed him. Somebody was probably calling on their girl. Other people enjoyed themselves, and he had Blakely riding him until he was crazy. He cursed the day he had ever joined the Army until he was breathless.

He started to retrace his steps when his eye caught the dark blotches in the snow. One was beside a buggy wheel, and the other a couple of yards from it. They looked odd there, and he thought about it. It was only a few more steps. Maybe he ought to see what it was.

The sight of Blakely cleared his head. He stood over him, and the gloating was the sweetest thing he had tasted in a long time. Somebody had pounded the Captain senseless. He moved to the other form and looked at it. He felt no pity. That was the one who had caused him all this trouble. It looked as though they had beaten each other unconscious, and he chuckled deep in his throat. Let them stay here and freeze to death. He didn't gave a damn.

He started to move on and saw Blakely's gun belt and tunic draped over a wheel. His eyes glistened. He had admired that dagger gun, but he had never dared hope he would ever own something like it. He could take it now, and Blakely would never know. He looked furtively about him, then eased the gun out of its holster. He thrust it under his coat, and his breathing was faster. He felt a heady sense of triumph. This night was really costing Blakely.

A thought struck him, and he hung in indecision. Blakely had that watch on him, and that was something else he had wanted. Take it, a small voice whispered. He's unconscious. What can he do?

Still fear held him. What if Blakely came to. That's why you'll always be a little man, Mahoney, the small voice said. You never take advantage of an opportunity.

It made up his mind. But to protect himself he pulled out the gun and held it in his right hand. Blakely hadn't better come to.

He kneeled beside the Captain, knowing a savage joy at the battered face. That would take some of the strut out of Blakely. It was awkward going through his pockets with his left hand, but he didn't dare transfer his weapon. That had to be ready in case Blakely stirred.

He found the watch in the second pocket and drew it out. He stared at it with greedy eyes. He would never know a finer night.

A hand clamped around his wrist, and Blakely stared at him. Mahoney thought he yelled, but his fear blocked all sound. It drove him into instinctive and defensive action, and the right hand hammered at Blakely's chest.

Blakely's chest arched convulsively, and sound rattled in his throat. His eyes looked as though they would pop out of his contorted face. Then he fell limply back. That last breath was a faint, sighing sound.

Mahoney wrenched the blade free. He stared at it with terrified eyes, and whimpering filled his throat. He hadn't meant to kill Blakely. Wasn't he only defending himself? The Army would shoot him for this; they wouldn't even let him begin to explain.

His first impulse was to break and run, and he forced himself into some rational pattern of thinking. He wasn't any worse off. Who knew he was here? If he threw the gun and watch away, who could ever connect him with this? It might be clearer thinking, but it didn't satisfy him. The Army had ways of finding things out, and it would be relentless in something like this. His eyes roved about in panic and swept across the unconscious man by the buggy wheel before the thought occurred to him. His breathing grew jerky as he developed the thought. Would the Army look for him, if he gave them somebody else. No! The Army would be satisfied. Now everything depended upon whether or not he could find a knife in the man's pockets. A sob rattled in his throat. Oh God, he was so close to safety. It couldn't be taken away from him now.

He searched through the second man's pockets, and satisfaction burst from him in a savage grunt as his hand closed on a pocket knife.

He straightened and opened it. Now he could keep the watch and dagger gun.

He walked back to Blakely and bent over him. The wound had almost stopped bleeding. He thrust the pocket knife's blade deep into it. The Army would have all the proof it would want.

He looked about him and could see nor hear any alarm. He moved quickly away into the night.

Gary stirred and groaned. His head was going to pound itself right off his shoulders. He raised a hand to it and felt the sticky wetness. His thoughts were vague, and he could get no solid hold on them. Then slowly, they clarified. Blakely must have hit him a powerful wallop to split his forehead like this. Then he remembered falling toward the wheel. Blakely hadn't done this. He must have hit his head on the rim. He tried to rise, and the strength wasn't there. He lay back and waited. He could make it in a little bit.

The sound of screaming tore through his skull. It was shrill and terrified, and it hurt his head as much as the pounding. He thought dully about it. What had happened to make somebody scream like that?

Chapter
FOUR

Gary admitted he was scared as he was led into the room where the court-martial was being held. He had been scared since the marshal had arrested him for Blakeley's murder. Elizabeth's screaming had awakened the neighborhood. He had been still trying to put things in order when a half-dozen men had seized him.

The marshal hadn't been interested in his story. "You tell it to the Colonel, Hobart. I'm turning you over to him."

That put the seed of an icy lump in Gary's stomach, and it had grown daily until it had become a solid mass of fear. The Colonel hadn't been interested in his story, either. "You'll get proper defense and a fair trial." But by the Colonel's grim look Gary had wondered just how fair the trial would be.

His assigned defense attorney was First Lieutenant Ben Halverson, and Gary didn't like the man. His face was long and cold, and the eyes seemed to have that same accusing look so many of the military eyes held. He had questioned Gary, and to Gary it sounded as though Halverson prejudged him.

"You admit you fought with him, don't you?"

Gary made no attempt to deny that. "But I didn't kill

34

him." How many times had he said that? And each time it seemed to get less attention.

"And you admit that it was your knife found in the Captain's body?"

"Yes." Gary had claimed it before he knew where it was found. "But I didn't kill him. I told you I knocked myself out in that fall."

Halverson angrily threw down his pencil. "You claim somebody else came along while you were unconscious and stabbed Blakely with your knife?"

"It has to be like that."

Halverson had stabbed a finger at him. "Mister, I'm going to give you some good advice. Throw yourself on the mercy of the court. It's the only chance you've got." His tone had said it was a damned slim one.

Gary had rejected the advice, and Halverson had shrugged. "It's your neck."

Now Gary's eyes were haunted as he looked at the seven officers behind the long table. Colonel Stenton, by reason of his rank, presided. The other members of the court ranged down to a lowly Second Lieutenant. Take away the age difference, and it was odd how much their faces looked alike.

Major Thomas was the trial judge advocate, and an anticipatory glint was in his eyes saying how hungry he was to be at Gary.

In answer to the Colonel's question, "How does the prisoner plead?" Halverson stood. "The prisoner pleads not guilty." He didn't actually shrug, but he gave the impression of it.

Thomas stood and went into his opening speech. He used ugly words such as murder and willfully and with malice, and they whirled around in Gary's mind. He kept glancing at Halverson, and Halverson's face was blank. Gary doubted he was even listening very attentively.

"Bring in your first witness," Stenton ordered.

Thomas nodded. "I call Sam Danfield."

The surprise was still on Gary's face as Danfield came into the room. Danfield hadn't seen that fight.

Danfield put apologetic eyes on Gary, then let them slide away. He swore to tell the truth, and sweat kept beading on his forehead. Yes, he was at the dance, but he hadn't seen any fight.

"Just answer the question," Thomas snapped.

Danfield squirmed in his chair, and Gary watched the red creep up from his collar. "Yes, sir."

"Was Mr. Hobart at the dance?"

"Yes, sir."

"And Captain Blakely?"

"Yes, sir."

"Did you see them talking together?"

Again, Danfield answered in the affirmative.

"Were they quarreling?"

Danfield twisted. "Hell, I don't know. I didn't hear anything they said."

"That will be all, Mr. Danfield."

Danfield's eyes touched Gary as he passed him and again slid away.

Gary's confusion was plain. What good did that do?

His confusion put a bleak smile on Halverson's face. "He established the fact there was contact between you and Blakely before the murder."

Thomas faced the Colonel. "I call Miss Elizabeth Danfield."

Gary visibly started. Why were they bringing her into this? She had no part in it. He started to rise to voice his

36

objection, and Halverson touched his arm in warning.

Elizabeth was plainly distraught. She twisted a handkerchief between her hands, and she wouldn't look at Gary.

Thomas escorted her to her chair, and his face was sympathetic. "I know how upsetting this is, Miss Danfield. But don't be nervous. Just answer my questions."

Elizabeth's nod was barely perceptible.

Thomas led her along smoothly. Yes, Mr. Hobart had taken her to the dance. She had danced with Captain Blakely, she didn't remember how many times.

"Did Mr. Hobart object? Please, a little louder, Miss Danfield."

Her voice raised. "Yes."

"Was he quarrelsome about it?"

Some flash of anger must have returned to her, for her head lifted. "He made a scene."

"Ah." Thomas sounded pleased. "An ugly scene, Miss Danfield?"

"Very ugly. People were watching us."

"Did he threaten Captain Blakely?"

Elizabeth searched her memory. "I don't remember. But he was very angry. He did tell me he would knock his head off, if he came near me again."

Thomas looked significantly at the Colonel. "And then what happened?"

"I demanded he take me home. My evening was ruined."

Thomas made that sympathetic, clucking sound. "Go on."

"I guess we quarreled. I didn't invite him to come in. I thought he had gone. But when I looked out later the buggy was still there. Then I saw two dark forms in the snow." She choked and couldn't go on for a moment.

"When I went out, both of them were unconscious. Then I saw the knife in Captain Blakely's chest. I screamed—" She broke down and covered her face with her handkerchief.

Thomas patted her shoulder. "Now, now. I know it has been an ordeal. But it's over." He glanced at Halverson. "No more questions."

Halverson shook his head. "No questions."

Gary turned his head to watch Elizabeth being led from the room. Her head was bent. She hadn't said a word that wasn't true, but it still shocked him. She had sounded as though she believed he was guilty.

Halverson tried to prevent it, but Gary insisted upon taking the witness chair. Somebody had to listen to his story.

Thomas was brutal in his examination. Gary kept shouting it didn't happen like that, that Thomas was twisting it. No, he didn't like Blakely. Yes, he was mad at him but not enough to kill him.

Thomas' eyes stabbed into him. "But you were furious enough to fight with him."

"I was. But he forced it. His pride wouldn't take what had happened."

"It was a hard fight?"

Gary considered that.

"The marks on your face show it."

"It was a hard fight. He kneed me and almost put me out. He clawed me. Then I knocked him out. I was pretty beaten up. I slipped and fell into a buggy wheel. I guess I hit my head on the rim." He unconsciously touched the bandage on his forehead. "I didn't come to until I heard Elizabeth—Miss Danfield screaming."

Thomas' face turned savage. "That isn't quite the way it happened, Mr. Hobart. Are you trying to tell us

38

that you knocked a much bigger, stronger man unconscious? Isn't it true that you were losing and pulled out the knife? That you stabbed Captain Blakely? Perhaps with your last remnant of strength. In your own words you say, 'I was pretty beaten up'. You tried to reach your buggy to get away. But the beating was too much for you. You fell unconscious."

Yelling, Gary was on his feet. "It wasn't that way. I told you the truth."

Stenton banged furiously with his gavel. "I demand order," he roared.

Halverson dragged Gary back into his chair. "You're making it worse."

Thomas looked at Gary, then shook his head in a false, pitying gesture. "No more questions."

Halverson repeated it, and this was no longer a nightmare; it was real, it was happening. Nobody believed him.

Thomas faced the court. "The prosecution rests, Sir."

Halverson stood. "We have no witnesses, Sir. The defense rests."

Gary stared at him in horror. Halverson was making no effort; he had never intended making any. He moved through the rest of it in a daze. He was led from the room while the court deliberated. It seemed that he was hardly out of the room before he was led back into it.

Stenton's face was cut out of granite with just about as much feeling in it. He didn't raise his voice, but his words were hammer blows, beating Gary to the floor. "Guilty as charged. The sentence is death. You will be shot the day after tomorrow. And God have mercy on your soul."

Gary forced an iron control upon himself. He could easily break into a screaming madman. He wanted to call all of them liars. He wasn't the murderer. But every one of them was.

Halverson shook his head. "I tried to warn you."

Gary's eyes blazed. "You bastard. You filthy bastard."

Halverson flushed, then turned and strode away.

The two guards took Gary by each arm, but there was no resistance in him. You did it, Elizabeth, he thought. You may not have meant to, but you did it.

Chapter
FIVE

If a man wants to learn how fast time can fly, let him face a death sentence. Minutes compress into the tiniest ticks of time and hours into minutes. And his thoughts turn into rat teeth that gnaw remorselessly. Worst of all was the completely helpless feeling, the all aloneness. Gary must have walked miles in the cramped confines of his cell. Two steps, wheel abruptly, then back two. If there was only something he could do. A million schemes of escape ran through his mind; the majority were inadequate; the remainder downright foolish.

The guard, outside the cell, looked in through the small, barred window and grinned. "You're gonna wear yourself out. You're gonna be so tuckered the firing squad will have to carry you out so they can shoot you."

Hackins had been on guard, and he had a vicious streak in him. Or maybe it was just the callow insensitivity of callow youth, for he was only eighteen. He spent his tour of duty trying to get a response out of Gary, and he looked in every few minutes.

"Yes, sir," Hackins continued. "The Colonel would be plumb mad if something happened to you before he could shoot you. I wouldn't want to make the Colonel mad. I've got to take awful good care of you."

Gary would have given about everything for one good

swing at him. He knew better than to pay any attention to him. Anything he could say would make Hackins pour it on that much worse.

His lack of response put anger in Hackins' voice. "You'll be talking in the morning, Mister. When they put all them rifles on you, you'll be begging and yelling. Who in the hell wants to talk to you anyway?"

He resumed his slow, measured treading, and Gary wanted to yell against the sound. Hadn't he already listened to that beat for an eternity?

The light was fading; it must be getting near dusk. The sounds of the normal life of the post drifted to him. He heard a horse gallop by, and a voice bawled in hoarse anger. A snatch of laughter was gone as quickly as he caught it. All that life out there was the same as it had been yesterday, and tomorrow would see no change. But his had stopped; it only needed a small detail to make it actually so. That hard, vicious twist seized his guts again. He had so many things he wanted to do; he hadn't really gotten started. He had to keep a tight hold against these kind of moments, or they would send him into something he would be ashamed of. He made his mind blank again and listened to the outside noises.

The wheels of a heavy wagon rumbled by. It must not have gone very far, for the wheel noise stopped. By thinking about the wagon, nothing else could enter his mind. That must be one of Danfield's freight wagons, making a delivery to the post. This should be about the last stop of the day, for it was getting late. Gary could imagine how impatient the driver must be to finish the day.

He was filled with bitter envy as he thought about that driver. After he finished here, drove back to town, un-

42

hitched and fed the teams, he would be heading home. His eyes widened as the thought slammed at him. If he could reach that wagon, the driver might take him off the post. It depended upon how thorough the inspection was at the gate. Logic said it was hopeless longing, but it might be done, if he could only get out of this cell. It had to be through the cell door, for he had thoroughly checked the small cell window. The door was the only hope.

He stretched out on the hard bunk and waited for Hackins' next stop at the small window. He sensed rather than saw him there. He let out a long, hollow groan and writhed.

Hackins cackled in amusement. "You got a belly pain thinking about tomorrow?"

Gary groaned again, and his convulsions grew worse. "Help me. Oh God, help me."

"What's wrong with you?" Hackins wasn't amused now.

"I don't know. It's tearing me to—" Gary's voice faded into a long moan. He twisted and jerked and fell onto the floor. His body threshed about like a headless chicken. He flopped on his stomach and lay still. The next few minutes would tell him if he was successful. It all depended upon whether or not Hackins yelled for help. An older, more experienced soldier would. But Gary was counting on this one's youth.

"Hey, get up." That was the start of alarm in Hackins' voice.

Gary made his breathing as feeble and shallow as he could, afraid that even the robust sound of it would arouse suspicion. He lay there until the sorrowful thought filled his head. It wasn't going to work; it wasn't going to draw Hackins into the cell. He tried to console himself by thinking, he was no worse off than he had been. He hadn't lost anything. Just his life.

He heard something squeak, and he didn't have to fake the catch in his breathing. That sounded like a key being turned in a lock. Now time had leaden feet it couldn't lift. He aged ten years before he heard the heavier sound of door hinges. He counted every footstep as they crossed to him. There couldn't be that many; the cell wasn't that big. Then something bored into his back, something that couldn't be anything else but a rifle muzzle.

"I'll beat your damned head off, if you're trying to pull something on me." That was worry in Hackins' voice. Colonel Stenton wanted this man shot. And the Army's wrath always landed on somebody, regardless of whether or not they earned it. The prisoner had gotten sick while under his guard. In some way, he would be blamed.

Gary thought that muzzle was going through him. If he made the slightest movement, the bullet would. He was rigid with suspense. How long could a man live under it without breaking into a thousand pieces?

He felt the muzzle pressure ease. If he was guessing right, Hackins should put a hand on his shoulder to turn him over. A rifle's length made it an awkward weapon in close quarters. Hackins would have to lift and hold it out to bend closer to him.

"Goddamn you," Hackins muttered and placed his hand on Gary's shoulder.

Gary twisted and came up off the floor both hands snaking for the throat. He had to make his first attempt good. If he missed clamping off an outcry, or had a bad struggle to subdue Hackins he was lost.

He saw the bulging of fear in Hackins' eyes, and that

44

first squawk of fear was only the forerunner of a greater outcry. Hackins made a mistake. He fought to bring his rifle into play, ignoring the protection of his throat.

Gary's hands clamped about his neck, and the thumbs dug into the vulnerable hollow at the base of the throat. He pulled Hackins to the floor and rolled over on top of him. He saw the distended eyes and the darkening color in the face. Nails clawed at his wrists, trying to pull his hands away. Gary didn't ease that deadly pressure. He didn't want to kill, but he could risk no quick return to consciousness. He wanted to stop on the borderline, and that was difficult to judge.

He heard the heels quit drumming, and the eyes looked as though they were ready to pop out of the head. He tentatively eased up, and the head lolled to one side. He removed his hands, and there was no stirring in Hackins. He bent his head close and listened. He blew out a soft sigh when he heard the faint and reedy fluttering of breathing.

He didn't know how long the unconsciousness would hold, and he had to do something to keep Hackins from giving an alarm too quickly.

He tore off a sleeve of his shirt and stuffed it into Hackins' mouth. He used the other one to tie it into place. He used his belt to tie the hands behind the back, binding the leather as tightly as he could. It wouldn't hold against a determined effort to be free, but it could give him a vital few minutes before Hackins' hands could jerk the gag out of his mouth.

He looked out of the cell window, but its small size gave him too limited a range. He reached down and picked up the rifle. A man with a rifle was a normal sight on any Army post. If somebody tried to stop him, would he use it? He would face that, if and when it arose.

He took a deep breath and eased out of the door. The light was fading rapidly, and he was grateful for that. The compound was almost deserted, and he could thank the supper hour for that. Across the compound, a sentry walked his endless beat, and there was another at the front gate. The wagon wasn't forty yards from him, and his relief came out in a small sighing sound. He wanted to break and run for it, but that kind of motion would call attention to him quicker than anything else. He forced himself to an even walk, and his skin was stretched tight in anticipation of a yell of discovery.

The wagon was backed up before a building, its tail gate down. There was no one around it, but from the building he heard fragments of sentences and a burst of laughter.

He took a deep breath and stepped into the wagon, bending low because of the canvas-covered bows. Some fortune was smiling on him, for the wagon was only about half emptied. Evidently, everything in it wasn't for the post. He dashed the hopes of that by thinking, or they haven't finished unloading.

The boxes were of different sizes and not packed in too tightly. He crawled over the tops of them until he found a space where he could wriggle in between two. He huddled there, holding his breath in fear the unloading would begin again.

The fear weakened when he heard a voice say, "Sarge, sign this damned paper so I can get out of here."

"What's your hurry, Lucas? We're not going anywhere."

Gary knew Lucas Steele. He was one of Danfield's drivers.

"But I am," Lucas growled. "My old woman will have supper waiting for me."

The Sergeant held up the signing, kidding Lucas a little longer. And Gary slowly died. Had Hackins revived, was he struggling even now to free his hands?

He heard the tail gate slammed into place, and the hooks fastened. "See you next trip, Lucas." Gary tried to make himself smaller. The voice sounded right over him.

"Sure, Sarge." Lucas walked to the front of the wagon, his whistling making every step.

Gary heard the brake kicked off and Lucas' yelled "Ho," followed by the pop of a whip. He was limp and exhausted when the wheels began turning.

He had one more bad spot—the front gate. He had to hope that Lucas was too well known to even be stopped. The wheels had been turning for a long time. Surely, they were off of the post by now.

His heart plummeted when he felt the wagon stop. A voice said, "What did you steal from us this time, Lucas?"

Lucas's voice had humor in it. "Nothing. Everybody watches me too closely."

The first speaker laughed, and Gary heard footsteps coming to the rear of the wagon. Should he make a break for it—or should he wait and pray that the inspection would be perfunctory? He weighed the odds and decided against the break. He would be on foot, and they would quickly run him down.

The voice came again. "I don't see anything that belongs to us, Lucas. You're an honest man up to here."

Gary breathed again when the wagon started. Now he could dare to believe he had made it. He was off of the post. He could drop off of the wagon any time he chose. Not too soon, he thought. Let it carry you out of sight, anyway.

47

He sat there, rocking with the lurching of the wagon. He would have argued with anybody who said the wheels weren't singing to him.

He looked out through a rent in the canvas. They were approaching town. He could leave the wagon any time he chose. Maybe it would be better to wait until they were in town. He had to have a horse, even if he had to steal one.

He peered out again, and the wagon was less than a block from Priam's stable. He would drop off in front of it and dart inside. Priam would help him.

He moved to the rear of the wagon and waited a few more seconds. He was in motion the moment his feet touched the street. He ran for the entrance and stopped just inside it. Emotion had put that panting in him; the physical exertion hadn't been nearly enough. He looked out, and the street was empty. The wagon rolled steadily down the street. Lucas hadn't noticed anything. He turned toward Priam's office.

Priam's jaw sagged when he saw him. "My God, Gary." He said it again as though his mind was empty of all else.

"I broke out, Priam." Sometime, he would tell Priam the details. He wondered if the Army had discovered it yet. He thought he saw a doubt in Priam's face. "I didn't kill him, Priam."

Priam stared at him, then nodded. "All right. If you say so. But they'll be looking for you."

Gary could bet on that. But he had a little time to think about his next step, a little room in which to take it.

"I could eat, Priam. My appetite wasn't so good back there."

"I imagine," Priam said dryly. "I got some bread and cold meat."

He set it out before Gary, and Gary had never tasted food so good. He finished and wiped his mouth with his hand. "I've got to have a horse, Priam."

"Bullet's still here."

Gary shook his head in awe. Everything had worked out for him tonight.

"Gary, where will you go?"

"To the ranch first and pick up a few things I need." He couldn't stay there long. That would be one of the first places they would look.

He jerked his head around at the sudden pounding of hoofs in the street. He ran to the entrance and peered out. The army patrol was already beyond the livery stable. God pity any pedestrian who got in their way. Hackins had freed himself in pretty short order at that.

He moved back to Priam. "They're looking for me. They probably figured Danfield's wagon had something to do with me getting off of the post. They'll look over his place first. It changes my plans. I won't go to the ranch."

He wouldn't even tell Priam where he was going. He would head for the breaks, that inaccessible, broken land that even lawmen avoided. But he couldn't leave now, not while an army patrol stomped around.

"Priam, do you think you can hide me until after midnight?" Honest men would be tiring by then and ready for sleep. He no longer belonged in that class, and it felt odd to think about.

Priam bobbed his head. "You get in the hay pile. If they do look here, they'll have to tear the pile apart to find you. You got no hand gun?"

Gary shook his head.

"Wait a minute." Priam hurried to his office. He came back and handed Gary an old Paterson Colt.

Gary hefted it in his hand. Its long five-and-a-half inch barrel made it heavy. He would have preferred his Peacemaker, a thirty-year younger gun, but this was sure better than no gun at all.

He thrust it into his waist band and hunted for something to say that would express how he felt. Thanks wasn't nearly enough for what Priam was doing. He punched Priam on the upper arm. Right now, that would have to do.

Chapter
SIX

To a man on the run, whatever the reason, the first few hours are the acute, strained ones. His sense of evaluation has to be changed, for he is in a completely different world. Gary would never forget how getting out of town had drawn him thin. Very few lights were on, and though he knew only an occasional person was up, he had the feeling that eyes watched him from every door and window. He led Bullet out of town, using the shadows of the buildings to cover him as long as he could. His nerves were as taut as fiddle strings, and with every breath he expected the first outcry of discovery. He called most of the people in this town friends, and he wondered what he would do, if any of them tried to stop him. The thought briefly entered his head; would he shoot them, if they tried to stop him? He didn't know the answer to that, and he wouldn't until he came up against it.

He covered the three blocks that it took to reach the town's outskirt, and nothing happened to break the silence. He neither saw nor heard any sign of the patrols, and that was his biggest relief. He had no doubt that Stenton would still have them out, but by now, they should have moved on beyond town. While he had hidden in Priam's haystack, he had heard a patrol search the livery stable. He cowered before a probing fork, but it hadn't gone deep enough. His face had been dripping wet by the time the patrol had gone. He had stayed in the haystack until Priam called him out in a low voice.

"Nothing stirring in town, Gary," Priam had said.

Gary nodded. The time had been long enough for a patrol to reach his place, and it put a hard, bleak cast in his face.

"Are you getting out of town now, Gary?"

Priam had an inordinate amount of anxiety in his face, and Gary thought he knew the cause. It would go hard for Priam if Stenton learned he had any part in this. He wiped away the disloyal thought. Priam had done enough to prove where he stood in this.

Priam went on at Gary's nod. "It's probably your best move, Gary. I just looked out and didn't see a soul on the street. I've got a few things for you to take."

He handed him an old worn sheepskin coat, and Gary slipped into it. It was blackened and stiff from long wear, but it still had some use in it, and Gary welcomed its warmth. He dropped the old pistol into his pocket. He wished he had brought his rifle with him tonight, but he hadn't, and Priam couldn't help him there. But the blanket was good. The last item was a small packet of food, and Priam said, "I wish it was bigger, but I ain't got any more in the place."

Gary laid his hand on his shoulder and let the gesture talk instead of words. Priam had done everything he could for him.

He saddled Bullet as Priam looked outside again. Bullet snorted and shied, and Gary didn't blame him, for this was no hour for man or animal to be going out.

Priam came back. "She's quiet."

Gary thrust out his hand. Priam took it, and neither man spoke. Neither had to, to know how the other felt.

Gary moved out of town at a slow walk, keeping hoof beat to a minimum. He mounted after he passed the town's last building. Once, he had thought of this town as his own, but that was gone now. Except for a few individuals, the town would be aligned with the army in this. The weather wasn't the source of the shiver that ran through him.

"Bullet, we're lucky so far," he said, and the horse's ears twitched forward and back as though he understood.

Gary kept the horse into that ground-eating lope, and the only tracks he saw were the ones his mount made. The fact that the snow wasn't marked didn't lull him into a false assurance. At any time he could cut the trail of one of those patrols.

He looked back, and the few lights of the town had faded. It gave him an odd, deserted feeling, and the loneliness wrapped about him. He was dull-eyed and haggard by dawn. The day hours would bring him more peril, and he looked for a spot in which to hole up until the night again gave him cover. He rode another mile before he found it. The small cave entrance, halfway up the bluff, looked like what he wanted.

He left Bullet on the bottom of a deep coulee and put him on a long tether. He watched Bullet paw down through the snow. Fore hoofs uncovered last summer's dried grass. Snow would have to be deeper than this to keep the horse from reaching it.

He looked back after he had walked a half-dozen steps. He could hear Bullet's sound of moving about, but he couldn't see him. The same would be true of a passerby, chancing to come this way. They would have to ride the brink of the coulee before seeing Bullet. A horse was difficult to hide, and Gary grimaced at the thought. But it was the best he could do.

He carried his saddle and saddle blanket to the cave. He had to get down on hands and knees to crawl into it, and he caught the old, musty smell. The smell told him that no animal was using it, at least, for some time. The cave was ideal for his purpose. It faced the right way, and it would keep the wind's teeth off of him.

He could sit up, and that was about all. He ate only enough of his food to take the edge off of his sharp hunger. He used both blankets to cover him and rested his head on the saddle. The rocky soil made for an uncomfortable bed. No matter which way he turned, one of those rocks gouged him. He was afraid cold would keep him awake, and if that didn't, thinking about food would. But he was wrong. The demands he had put on his body were a heavy club, and it hammered him into oblivion.

He slept through most of the day's hours, and when he awakened, he had to stare about him to realize where he was. Last night rushed back at him and oriented him fast enough. He had jumped from one world to another, and this one filled him with fear.

He ate some of his food, stopping long before he wanted to. His stomach growled, and he tried to ignore it. He crawled out of the cave and stood, and his muscles cried out a different kind of protest. He whipped his arms and stamped his feet to return circulation to them. He swore as the fiery needles pierced his arms and legs, and he kept up the movement until the needles vanished.

Bullet had beaten down all the snow and eaten the grass in the radius of the tether rope. Gary removed the pin and led him to a spot that wasn't trampled. He would not ride until dark, and Bullet could graze until then. He watched Bullet crop at the grass and wished his supply of food was as assured as Bullet's was.

With the darkness, he saddled Bullet. "It's time to go, boy." A man, by himself, got hungry to hear the sound of a human voice. Maybe he was lucky that Bullet couldn't answer him back. Or he would have expressed what he thought about this night riding.

Gary rode through the second night, and he thought it wasn't quite as cold as last night. The big thaw could come at any hour, and when it did, the snow would vanish in a hurry. He didn't look back at his trail as often as he had before, for repetition had dulled the edge of fear's teeth. He thought mostly about food. Riding only at night, it was probably that he wouldn't even see game, and he was afraid to hunt by daylight. If somebody didn't see him, the sound of a gun report would carry for a long way. That would have to wait until he reached the breaks. He would be out of food before then.

He was right about that. The food was gone when he rode into the breaks shortly after the third dawn. He looked out over the rough country with weary eyes. Three classes of men lived in this country—if he knew where to look for them. The wolfers, outlaws, and rustlers all lived in the breaks. The wolfers skinned wolves for their living, and the law didn't have the interest in them they had in the outlaws and rustlers. The second two classes were wanted men, but no law authorities dared to search in the breaks. Fifty men could stumble about in them and never know how many unseen pairs of eyes watched them.

This was his country now, Gary thought. He was relatively safe here. He shook his head. He wouldn't be safe, if he didn't get food.

His eyes swept the country again. This land lay in

twisted folds, canyons and upheavals, overpowering a man's spirit until he felt no bigger than a speck. Canyons and coulees, all sizes, stretched into the hazy horizon, and the serrated, broken backbones buttressed the canyons.

He hadn't the slightest idea where to find men who lived here. He knew shacks were in this land, built by outlaws and rustlers, but they would be hard to find. There was even a small collection of shacks, that was called Carroll, but he didn't know which way to turn. He thought wryly, if he could find them, they should take him in; he was one of them now. He badly needed what charity he could talk out of them; he was out of food and money.

He looked behind him; for the last time he would worry about that direction. He saw no movement behind him. He could forget the Army, though he had no doubt that the patrols were still out. Gary doubted Stenton would send them into the breaks. Stenton would dislike entering it as much as did the civilian law officers.

He let Bullet make his own pace, and he kept his eyes open for any kind of tracks in the snow. The flat, pancake-shaped chinook clouds were forming over the hills, and that meant a thaw coming today. Before the day was over, water would puddle in the depressions and begin to trickle in the coulees.

He saw not the slightest kind of track, and he cursed this huge, empty country. Then his eyes gleamed. That was rabbit track standing out vividly in the snow. He pulled Bullet down to a walk, and his eyes traced the tracks ahead of him. They stopped at a bush, and for a moment, he couldn't see the rabbit. Then, there it was, in the middle of the bush, its winter white standing out starkly against the vivid tracing of the bush.

His hand shook as he pulled the pistol from his pocket,

and he forced it steady as he aimed. It was a fairly long shot, and if he missed, a running shot would be almost impossible.

He closed his eyes against the watering, then reopened them. He squeezed the trigger, and with the report, the rabbit lunged. For a dreadful moment, he thought he had missed, then the rabbit was kicking in the snow.

Gary dismounted and ran toward him. He picked up the animal by its back legs. He hit it with the pistol barrel, just behind the ears, and the rabbit was still. He stood there, looking at it. It didn't seem very big.

He skinned the animal, and the carcass looked even smaller. Hunger had a trick of keeping water in his mouth. Dry wood was hard to find, and he searched under the over-hang of rocks and dirt banks. He shook the snow off of sticks and wiped them on his pants. He thought it would be dry enough to light it. He used the smallest of twigs at first, lit them, and nursed them with slow care. He sighed as the first tiny plume twisted away and the fire slowly strengthened.

He impaled the carcass over a stick and held it close to the flames. He slowly turned it, seeing the juices bubble out and drip into the flames. The grease gave more vigor to the fire. He held the meat over the fire until it burned out. He knew it hadn't been long enough to cook it through, but that didn't bother him.

He tore off a leg, and he was right. The meat wasn't cooked clear to the bone. He wanted to wolf it, and he forced himself to chew each mouthful thoroughly. The rawness didn't bother him. He gnawed each bone before he tossed it aside. When he finished, most of his hunger was satisfied.

He caught up Bullet, and the cleared area of snow said that the horse had done better than he had. He mounted, and his eyes searched the land. He had four bullets left, and they wouldn't carry him far, even if his remaining shots were as successful. The snow covered all evidence of a trail, but if he was going to make one, it would be one at the base of the hills. He put Bullet into a faster walk.

Chapter
SEVEN

As he rode, his face was sober under the weight of his thoughts. The meal of rabbit wouldn't carry him far. He watched for two things; tracks of small game and any indication that would point out a trail. It's emptiness mocked. It was a wild, desolate land, and it seemed to carry little of animal or man.

Last night's lack of sleep was beginning to catch up with him, and he had to keep fighting its encroaching grip. He kept Bullet moving through the miles. He no longer feared the daylight except for its emptiness. He needed game of any kind, or he would spend a hungry night.

With the sun's climb, he felt the increased heat of its rays. He unbuttoned the sheepskin and let it ride down off his shoulders. By tomorrow, big patches of the snow would be gone.

It was mid-afternoon when he stopped Bullet to let him graze. He picked out an elevation to make another survey. For a moment, he thought he would see what he had seen the other times; failure. Then he saw the four figures. They were a good way off, too small for him to make out details about them, but close enough for them to hear a gun's report. At the moment, they were heading diagonally away from him, and he had to stop them.

He pulled the pistol from the coat pocket and pointed it skyward. Then a warning instinct checked him. He didn't know who they were; Army patrol, or law party.

He argued against the warning; he was deep in the breaks, and the chances were in his favor that those four didn't belong to either part. His finger closed on the trigger twice.

The reports carried to them, for he saw them stop. He was well aware of how many shells he had left. If those figures meant him bad, he couldn't do a lot about it.

He started Bullet moving again. He breathed a sigh as he neared them. He thought he had never seen them before, but their clothing told what their occupation was. He had seen wolfers in Benton, and all of them had a same cast about them. They wore clothing until it was so dirty and grease-stained that it became uniform garb with them. The wind blew over them, and as he approached he could smell the rank smell of the garments. He wasn't objecting, he was too relieved to find them.

"My God, I'm glad to see you."

The man, who answered him, was so blocky that it made him appear shorter than he was. He wore an old buffalo robe coat, the hair falling out in patches, making it look mangy. "Do you rush a man with a pistol in your hand?"

Gary had forgotten about carrying it, and he grinned. "I'd forgotten it." He dropped the pistol into his pocket. "Those two shots I fired cut me down to two shells."

If he had any other thought in mind, it wouldn't do him any good; not against three rifle muzzles trained on him. Some of his relief was tempered with worry. He couldn't say hostility was in them, but he certainly didn't see any friendliness.

"What are you doing here?" The same man spoke to him. He had the manner of authority, and Gary would say the role was natural to him. He had a massive beard, and his hair was liberally splashed with gray. The eyes were a startling blue, as hard and cold as winter ice. The face was hewn out of granite, and exposure had had its part in fashioning it. But that wasn't all of it. Something inner had part of the making of that hardness. One cheek was pouched out, and the man spat an amber stream of tobacco juice into the snow.

Gary tried to smile as the increased worry gnawed on him. "I'm lost. And out of food and ammunition."

His eyes ran over the others. It hit him with a shock that one of the four was a woman. He would say she hadn't yet reached twenty, but her face had an unusual maturity. Her hair was coarse and black, but it wasn't dull when the light caught it at the right angle. That and the duskiness of her complexion said there was Indian blood in her. If so, the two bloods blended well. The clothes made her look bulky, but she still gave an appearance of suppleness. The bones in her face had been sculped in fine lines and the flesh molded well over them. He wondered if those black eyes ever looked soft. They didn't now. She openly stared, but it wasn't friendliness nor curiosity that motivated her. If he had to name the emotion behind those eyes, it would be dislike if not hating.

He saw the glance exchanged among them. It angered him. He had said his need as simply as he could, it hadn't meant a thing to them.

The biggest of the three men grinned with malice. "Are we supposed to worry about that?" He was a head taller than the others, and he had width of shoulder and chest to go with it. His nose had been flattened in some

61

past brawl, and there was a mean look to his eyes. "Are you worried about it, Hanks?"

Hanks shifted in his saddle. "I won't sleep over it tonight." He had a wizened face, and he looked tougher than an oak knot. The flash of his teeth had a feral cast to them. "I'll let you worry over it, Ruch."

The woman hadn't expressed an opinion on this, and Gary didn't count her anyway. Out of the three men, two of them were openly against him. The sun didn't seem as bright as it had been, and the wind's bite seemed to be sharper. What kind of men turned down a request like that? The blocky man seemed familiar to him, and something in his mind picked at him, then he had it. He had contacted Curdy briefly over three years ago. He wondered if Curdy remembered it at all. He wished he had a stouter prop to bolster his assurance.

"I know you," he said. "Hale Curdy. I ran across you three years ago while I was hunting strays. I put a rope on your horse and yanked it out of the quicksand."

He saw the memory touch Curdy's eyes. Curdy would have lost his horse without Gary's help. He had ridden away without expressing thanks, and Gary hadn't expected it.

Curd's eyes remained opaque. He was a hard man to read. "I remember." He gave Gary no help, either with expression or words.

"I'm Gary Hobart." Did the name mean anything to Curdy?

It did, for Curdy's eyes turned more speculative. "The man who killed that Army captain. A drifter passed through our camp yesterday afternoon. He said that was all Benton talked about. So you're the one."

"I didn't kill Blakely. I got knocked out. When I came to, somebody had stabbed him. I was blamed for it."

It didn't change the weighing in Curdy's face. "Now that's right interesting. Why should I believe you? And how in the hell did you get away from them?"

"What's the use of listening to him," Ruch put in impatiently. "I say we divvy up his things. I'm putting in my bid for his horse."

Gary's eyes switched to him, and a shiver ran through him. The big bastard meant it. He wouldn't be cold before they started cutting him up.

Hanks nodded an eager agreement to Ruch's words. "Maybe the Army's offering a reward for him."

Curdy chewed off a bite of a plug. "Shut up, you two. Not so fast."

Gary's hopes revived. Two of them were openly against him. Curdy's stand wasn't as definite. Maybe that favor had stuck in his mind.

"I tried to tell them at the trial what had happened. They wouldn't listen. They judged me with minds already made up. I overpowered a guard and slipped out in a freighting wagon. They didn't discover I was gone until I was off the post."

How well he remembered those long minutes in the courtroom. There had been no justice in them. He wondered if that youthful sentry had recovered from that choking. Whether or not he had wouldn't make any difference to the army.

He kept his attention focused on Curdy, hoping to see an indication of what he had in mind. "I got into the breaks as fast as I could make it. I was glad to run into you."

Ruch's teeth were a white slash in the blackness of his beard. "Maybe you won't be."

Anger showed in Curdy's face. "I told you to shut up, Ruch. Since when do you make the decisions?"

63

Ruch glowered at him, but he kept his mouth shut. Curdy switched back to Gary. "Your shots stopped us. We were heading back to camp when you stopped us."

Gary's heart sank. Curdy's words explained nothing; at least, in Gary's favor. Bitterness was in his voice. "So that reward sounds good to you."

Curdy pursed his lips as though he reflected on it. When he spoke, he wiped Gary's bitterness away. "I'm not interested in anything they could offer. I've got no love for the army. And I had none for Blakely. I ran into him last year, while he was on patrol. He acted as though I had to get his permission to breathe."

Gary's relief came out in a small sigh. That said it plain enough for anybody to understand how Curdy felt. But it didn't suit the other two; it was written all over them.

They won't jump Curdy, Gary thought. At least, not for the moment. The girl's face hadn't changed. It probably didn't matter how she felt. She, like the other two would take Curdy's orders. What was her relationship to Curdy? His wife? It could be, even though the age span between them was wide. Gary didn't miss the way Ruch's eyes ran over her at every opportunity. Curdy was crazy to keep a woman around Ruch.

"If I could get some food and a few shells," he said, "I would be set up all right."

Curdy seemed to give everything he said a maddening deliberation. "We might consider it. Let's ride."

He wheeled his horse and looked back at Gary after a few steps. Gary hadn't moved. "Are you coming?"

Gary lifted his reins. He didn't have much choice in the matter.

The girl rode on Curdy's right. Again, Gary speculated about their relationship. She seemed to hover as close as she could to Curdy. Because of Ruch's eyes? Maybe. Gary looked at Ruch and saw the hot gleam he put on her. He thought, if the woman was his and Ruch looked at her like this, he would shoot him.

Ruch caught Gary watching him, and his face was tough. Gary hadn't exchanged a dozen words with him, but it didn't take much talk to fan a natural animosity between them.

He shrugged and moved Bullet beside Curdy. It was all Curdy's affair. He was aware of the undercurrents between these people. He almost wished he hadn't found them. The harsh hand of hunger twisted his stomach, and he let go of the thought.

He turned his head, and Ruch and Hanks rode behind him. The rifles were booted, but he remembered how those muzzles had looked, pointing at him. His backbone crawled. Did Curdy have enough authority over them to control them? Gary had been thrown into something that could flare into open hostility among the three men. He didn't want any part in it, but he had no part in the decision. He would take what supplies they would give him and go on his way. Was he relieved or not that he had found somebody in this barren, rough land? He wouldn't be able to answer that right now.

Chapter
EIGHT

The sun was dipping when Curdy said, "Camp ahead of us." He pointed at the shallow length of a bluff ahead of them.

For a moment, Gary saw nothing that broke the surface of the bluff, then he saw three uniform spaces that looked different than the drab soil. They were oblong in shape and tawny in color, and he guessed at what was behind them.

"Dugouts?" He turned a questioning face toward Curdy.

Curdy nodded. "Dug them last year. We finish up the season here because it's closer to the markets. A man never gets used to living in a hole. But it serves its purposes. You'll stay tonight with us."

Gary slowly closed his mouth on his protest. Curdy's words didn't leave him any room to argue.

He followed Curdy to the grove at one end of the bluff. He didn't see the wagon camp until he was well among the trees. Five wagons were among them, plus a dozen picketed horses. Curdy had picked his location well. A man would never know he was on it before he stumbled over it.

"We covered a hell of a swing this season," Curdy said, and some disatisfaction was in him. "Up in Canada and back again. Not long now, and it'll be over for another season."

Gary looked into a wagon as he rode by it. It was loaded with flattened pelts, baled and tied with pieces of rope. He had no idea of how many pelts were in it, but there had to be a goodly number. Those bales would be heavy and bulky to handle, and the stiffness had been frozen into them throughout the winter.

"It's been a good hunt," Curdy said. "Only one of the wagons isn't filled. We should be able to go through the rest of the month, if we don't get a lasting thaw. If it holds too long, it ruins the skins before we can get to them."

Gary knew how much traveling it had taken to gather all those skins. Wolfers went where the buffalo went, for the wolves followed them. He thought of the hardships wolfers withstood to make their harvest for the winter. He could see nothing for him in this business. A bleak thought followed on the heels of the first one. He didn't have anything to say about picking out any business he might want.

Curdy put his and the woman's horses on the picket line. "Go ahead, Dawn. I'll be right along."

Gary watched her move away. She had a smooth, flowing grace, and he repeated her name in his mind. It had a pleasant sound. Ruch and Hanks were staring at her, and Curdy caught it. The veins in his throat looked as though some inner rage swelled them.

But he didn't comment on it, and Gary let it die. Whatever Curdy wanted to do about it, if anything, was his business. This was part of the undercurrents Gary had first been aware of; but more open and deeper. He felt Curdy's veiled weighing of him and felt the irritation well up in him. Once more, he felt that Curdy wanted to pull him into something that he had in his head. It tightened his skin, and he would be relieved to get away from here as fast as he could.

"I'll get your horse a few oats after supper," Curdy said. "Ruch, Flackins, and Hanks have the end dugout. Summers and Tindle have the next one, Dawn and I the other. Summers and Tindle have room for you."

Gary hadn't seen Tindle and Summers. If they were like Ruch and Hanks, he didn't want to.

Curdy caught the unease in him and grinned. "They don't like Ruch and Hanks any better than you do. This is the first year Ruch and Hanks have hunted with us. It hasn't worked out too well. A man doesn't know another until he hunts a season with him."

Gary held back what he wanted to say. He needed food, and he was in no position to refuse staying the night. Fatigue pulled at him with heavy hands. He could spend a night in the dugout, then travel on in the morning.

He fell into step with Curdy toward the dugouts. Dawn had already disappeared behind the buffalo flap.

"It's a dirty, hard business," Curdy said. "Tempers flare under it, and a man gives up living except like an animal. But it can be profitable. Last season, I cashed almost two thousand dollars worth of skins." He shrugged as though the amount didn't mean too much. "It doesn't cost much for a man to live the rest of the year. But most of us spend everything we make in the saloons and gambling halls. After a couple of weeks, it's all gone. Then it's back to cutting wood for the steamers until the next skinning season. I don't know what keeps a man coming back to it—" He let it die, and that seemed to be a lost note in his voice.

Gary wondered what had driven Curdy into it. Every

man needed a solid goal, and wolfing didn't seem to be it; certainly not if the gains from it were thrown away in a riotous couple of weeks. "How long have you been at it?"

Curdy's face tightened as though the question refired some memory. "Four years. It seems like a hundred—" He left that unfinished, too. "You ready to eat?" His face cracked in a brief smile at the emphasis in Gary's nod.

He led Gary toward the middle dugout. "We were lucky these were empty when we got back to them almost a month ago. It makes for a shorter haul to Benton." He pushed aside the hanging buffalo robe and ducked to enter.

Gary did the same as he followed him. The buffalo robe hung over the entranceway. He could straighten inside but just barely. The enclosure was large enough for three men to stretch out on the floor and little more. It was crude shelter, and it must have been brutal during the coldest of the winter.

Two men were seated on old robes, and the hewn-out space had a close, fetid smell, the reek of unwashed men living together too long. A small, metal stove, its smoke vented out through a tin pipe that went up through the roof, was glowing red.

Curdy gestured at the two men. "Summers and Tindle. This is Gary Hobart."

They stared at Gary, and their faces expressed nothing. Both were average-sized men, dressed in the worn and filthy clothes of the wolfers. Most of their faces were covered with beard, but it didn't hide the suspicion in their eyes. What part of their faces showed had been marked heavily by weather and privation. These were men, living a lonely, hard existence.

"Hell, Hale," Summers said. "You're not letting him

69

join us this late and expect to share in the season." He puckered his lips and spat an amber stream at the dirt floor just beyond the robe.

His protest tickled Curdy, and he chuckled. "He's no worry to you. He wants a night's lodging and something to eat."

The sharp, pungent odor of tobacco juice drifted to Gary. He wasn't sure the suspicion left their eyes. They wouldn't be at ease with anybody who was different from them. A scar came up out of the beard line and bisected the cheekbone. Summers picked at it with an absent finger, and Gary wondered if the cold ever bothered him in it. The nail of the finger was rimmed with a permanent looking crescent of black.

"That puts a different light on it," Tindle drawled. The season's wearing was obvious in his ragged clothes, and it was hard to see how they hung on him. His lips were scabbed with chap sores, and Gary doubted that the man could be able to remember his last bath.

"You'd share a meal, wouldn't you, Summers?" Tindle's words contained a touch of humor. "Summer's doesn't want anybody cutting into his share. He wants only the chippies in Benton doing that."

They fell into wrangling with each other, and Gary's strain eased. He might get to know them a little better, if he stayed around them. One night was all he wanted of them.

"Both of you stay off of him," Curdy ordered. "He's just gotten away from the Army's reach." He moved toward the entranceway. "You know where to find me, if you want me."

The silence, after the robe fell behind him, held for several long minutes. That was new interest in them as

70

they studied him. "The one who killed that army captain?" Summers asked.

Gary nodded. So along with Curdy they had heard the drifter's story. "But I didn't kill him. They blamed me for it."

He met's Summers' eyes without flinching. Let the man think what he wanted about it.

"I got no love for them," Summers growled. "One of their Sergeants flattened me last spring. He had a dozen men with him and they caught me alone." The beating must have been severe, for rancor was still with him. He must have gotten a pleasure in Gary's affair, for he said, "Tell us how it happened."

Gary wasn't going to relate it for their amusement, and he snapped, "I don't want to hear any more about it."

A subtle change touched their faces. He was going to spend a night in this confined space with these two. It wasn't wise to turn them against him.

"It was a fight over a girl. He almost whipped me. But after I knocked him unconscious, I slipped in the snow and hit my head against a buggy rim. When I came to, my knife was sticking in him."

He thought that was doubt in their faces, and his eyes heated. "You don't believe it any more than my trial board."

"Not me," Tindle argued. "I was thinking it was too bad you didn't have the pleasure of sticking him."

A pot on the stove bubbled, and its aroma carried to Gary. It held the smell of some kind of cooking meat, and Gary's mouth watered.

"You hungry?" Summers asked.

"Yes." The single word expressed Gary's need.

71

Summers stood and moved to the stove. He un- sheathed a knife and poked around in the liquid with it. He stabbed a big chunk of meat and handed it on the knifepoint to Gary. It was hot enough to feel it in his fingers, and he paid no attention to it. He wolfed off a huge chunk and chewed, the pleasure of it filling his stomach.

"Man, you wanted that," Tindle said and handed him a piece of several-days-old squaw bread.

It was a crude, rough meal, but Gary had never tasted anything better. They sat cross-legged before the stove, and no talk broke up the moment. Now and then, one of them approached the stove to find a new chunk of meat. Gary smiled at both of them, and the dark, brooding eyes of Summers warmed and returned it. This eating of a shared meal had softened all of them.

Tindle offered him another piece of meat, and Gary waved it aside. He must have eaten for a solid thirty minutes, and he couldn't hold another bite. He patted his swollen belly. "I couldn't eat any more. I'm full up to the teeth."

"I can't offer you a cigarette," Summers said. "But I can give you a chew of tobacco."

Gary accepted the gnawed-on plug. Summers had dug it out of his pocket unwrapped, and it was covered with lint. It didn't hamper Gary's appetite for the tobacco.

He lay back on one of the robes and let the enjoyment of the tobacco taste take him. It was hotter in here than he first thought it. A man would be able to sleep in here without coat or blanket. He must have gotten used to the offensive smell, for it didn't bother him now.

"What did you do?" Tindle asked.

"Rancher." Gary's face tightened at the recall of the

memory. "I guess the Army's got everything I had. I'll get it back some day—" The belief wasn't strong enough for him to finish it.

"Maybe," Tindle grunted. "Did you meet Ruch and Hanks?"

"They were with Curdy when I found them." Anger stirred in Gary. "Ruch wanted to divide me up right there."

Tindle snorted. "He would. And he's big enough and rough enough to do it. I think he's a little afraid of Curdy. Or he wouldn't have kept his hands off of Dawn by now."

Gary thought about her for a moment. Tindle sounded as if he thought Curdy was crazy, too, to keep the woman around Ruch."

"His wife?"

Tindle stared at Gary with speculative eyes. "No, his daughter. If you've thoughts—"

"I haven't. I told you my fight was over a woman. She's still waiting for me."

"Good." Tindle pulled a bundled robe out of the rear corner of the dugout.

He spread it on the floor. "I can get you another one, if you think so."

Gary nodded his thanks. The echo of Tindle's words about Ruch was still in his head as he stood.

"Where are you going?" Tindle demanded.

"I told you that Ruch had an interest in my horse. I'm going out to see that Bullet's all right." It probably wasn't necessary that he be concerned. If Ruch intended taking the horse, this wouldn't be the time. The man would wait until the camp broke up for the end of the season.

"Don't let him push anything like a fist fight," Tindle advised. "He's a powerful bastard. If you get in trouble with him, shoot him."

Gary pulled aside the door flap. "I'll remember that."

A full moon had risen, and it glittered coldly on the snow. He moved toward the horses, thinking he was the only one outside, then he saw a darker shadow, standing at the picket line.

He moved noiselessly toward the shadow, letting its size mark it for him. Only one man in the camp could make a shadow that big, and Gary's anger rose and lodged in his throat. Some of that anger was directed at the horse. Bullet was fickle when it came to accepting attention, and Ruch's hands were all over him.

Gary drew a deep breath. "Get your goddamned hands off him." He followed the words with a rush. Tindle's advice had quite slipped his mind.

Chapter
NINE

Ruch turned, and he didn't have time to set himself. Gary slugged at the beard, and the bone beneath it was hard under his fist. Ruch's handling of his horse was a culmination of abuses during the past week, and Gary had to collect for it; he had to hurt this man.

Ruch staggered back several broken steps before he caught himself. He raised a hand to the hurt and stared at Gary. The moonlight was bright enough for Gary to see the wildness sweep into the man's face.

"Why damn you," Ruch howled and sprang forward. He had tremendous size and power had to be in it. But the speed was lacking. Gary easily escaped that first rush, slipping away from that clubbing blow.

He waited, poised on the balls of his feet, making the plan of his fight. He had learned considerably about Ruch's ability. He had strength but no skill, and he was slow of foot. Anger was still in Gary, but it was cold and thinking. Ruch could break him with one solid blow, but he didn't intend letting him have it. Gary doubted a half-dozen blows would put Ruch down. But each one would slow him that much. He would have to hit and run, letting the total of them drain the man.

His teeth bared mirthlessly. Maybe he had been a

damned fool to make this fight, but he needed it as a release for everything that had happened to him.

"Come on you, you big bastard."

Ruch roared with rage and lumbered forward. Gary let him reach him before he jolted him. He tried to put the punch on the Adam's apple. A successful blow there could hurt him badly, but the blow went in too high. It landed on the jaw again. It stopped Ruch and even rocked him back, but it didn't drop him.

Ruch yelled his fury again. If he kept on making that much noise, he would pull the others outside. He moved away from Ruch, making him travel steps that would wear at him. Gary didn't set himself to throw a blow. It cost him power by not hitting off a solid planting, but he couldn't afford the risk. Ruch's breathing began to sound as though there was fire in it.

Gary paused and sucked in gulps of air whenever Ruch let up the pressure on him. He hadn't been touched yet, but the need to keep away made a demand on his lungs.

He went back to the slow whittling, and his elusiveness baffled Ruch. He had swung until he was arm weary, and now he stopped, his face showing as much bewilderment as rage.

"Goddam you." Spittle ran down the corner of Ruch's lips. "Stop and fight."

"Come and get." Gary was far enough away from Ruch that he could come off his toes, and he felt the strain of the fight in his legs and arms. He had hurt Ruch, and it showed in every move of Ruch's. Ruch had come after him with every step, and now he sagged before Gary, his shoulders drooping, his arms hanging low. If Gary wanted to put him out, he had to go after him.

He darted in and before Ruch could raise those weary

arms, Gary stung him hard. He felt awe for Ruch. He had hit him a lot of times and never dropped him once.

Blood spattered from Gary's fist, and he was sickened of this fight, wanting it over. Ruch's fists could only paw feebly, and there was no coordinated movement in them.

Gary thought he could end it, and he sprang forward again, setting his feet solidly. He glided in between Ruch's pawing hands and hammered his fists into the face. He put his weight behind every blow, and Ruch rolled drunkenly before them. He grew careless, and it happened. Ruch clubbed him on an ear, and it put a loud ringing in Gary's head. He tried to move back to give his head enough time to clear. The snow had been thoroughly churned up and made slippery. His foot went out from under him, and his arms flailed to regain his balance. He fell and lit on his back, and the impact pumped the breath out of him. That watered his vision, and now he had to get out from under the heavy mass diving at him. He heard Ruch's triumphant yell and tried to roll to his left, hoping to slip from Ruch. He lacked the tiny space of time he needed. He didn't see Hale Curdy's hurrying up to the scene.

Ruch landed on him, knocking the last remnant of breath from him. He gasped as Ruch plowed him down into the snow. He landed astride him and slugged at Gary's face. Those jarring blows came one after another, and Gary couldn't put up a defense against them. The shock rocked throughout his body, and a blackness was crawling at him. Every time Ruch hit him, a red light exploded in that blackness. His struggling grew feebler, and he was beginning to slide toward the darkness.

The blackness didn't come any closer to him, and he thought about it with odd detachment. It occurred to him

77

that Ruch was no longer beating him, and he wondered about that, too. His thoughts were heavy footsteps in deep, clinging mud, and he couldn't get one free to examine it. It hit him with sudden unexpectedness that Ruch was no longer on him, that he was free of his weight.

He tried to roll over, to get his hands and knees under him, and he couldn't make it. He fell back, and his tortured lungs racked him with each breath.

"Can you get up?" The voice came to him from a long way off, and he had to think about it. He tried to put a name to the voice and couldn't. The answer was simple about him getting up; he couldn't.

Hands went under his armpits, and even with that help, he could barely stand. My God! He didn't know that simple act could take so much effort. He leaned against the man who had helped him up, and it took persistent effort to recall who he was.

"Gary, can you understand me?" Curdy asked.

Gary weakly bobbed his head. Things were getting clearer. They were also bringing a lot of pain with them.

"Where's Ruch?" he asked weakly.

"Lying over there. I couldn't pull him off of you. I knocked him off with a gun barrel."

Gary had to squint his eyes to firm Curdy's hazy outline. "I hope you knocked his damned head off."

"I tried to. I heard the noise you two made and came out. A man can kill an ox easier. All I did was knock him out. Did he break anything?"

Gary felt gingerly of his face, and it was bleeding. Ruch had marked him well. "I don't think so. I made a mistake and let him get hold of me."

"He did a job. What started it?"

Gary's head was clear, but it gave room for more pain to hit him. "He was pawing Bullet. I told him to keep his hands off. We got in an argument over it. I had him whipped, then I got careless."

Curdy glanced at Ruch. "He's coming to. Do you want more of him."

Ruch stirred and groaned. Gary winced as he looked at him. "Not tonight."

"Let him come to by himself," Curdy said unfeelingly. He put his shoulder under Gary's weight to help him. "Come on and let's look at what he did."

Gary stumbled along beside him. He hoped Ruch hurt as bad as he did.

Curdy held aside something for Gary to enter, and Gary didn't realize it was the robe over the entrance until he brushed against it. Curdy must be putting him back with Summers and Tindle. Gary didn't want to talk to them. All he wanted was to lie down.

"Dawn," Curdy ordered. "Light a candle and see what you can do for him."

Gary heard her moving about, then a candle made a small light. It hurt his eyes, as he realized Curdy had taken him to their dugout. Gary wearily thought about it. Why had Curdy taken his side? Nothing showed on the girl's face, and she probably wasn't too happy that he was here. He thought about her. The sound of her name, Dawn, was pretty.

Curdy took the candle from her. "Sit down."

Gary sank down to the floor. She looked as though she didn't see him, but her hands were deft and gentle. A wet cloth ran across his face again and again, and he had to keep his lips locked on an outcry.

She kept rinsing out the cloth, and the water, in the pan, slowly turned to a deep pink.

"Ruch did it," Curdy said to some unspoken question of hers. "Have you something to put on those cuts?"

Some fleeting emotion crossed her face, but she didn't answer. Gary thought irritably, does she ever talk?

She moved away, and when she came back, she spread something on his cuts and bruises. Its first touch stung, then the hurt eased.

He said his thanks, and she stared blankly at him. His irritation swelled. He wanted to get out of this dugout.

He stood, and he was stronger. He was also aware of every throbbing hurt.

"I'll go back with you," Curdy said.

Gary started to refuse him, then held it. Ruch might still be out there. Gary didn't want the fight starting again tonight.

He stepped outside and looked toward the spot where Ruch had been. Ruch was gone; he must have come to on his own, and that suited Gary just fine.

He owed Curdy thanks for stopping Ruch, and he put it into awkward words.

"I welcomed hitting him. I should have done it before." Curdy looked as though a rush of words was on his tongue, but he paused.

He reached out in some feeling and laid his hand on Gary's arm. "Stay with us until the hunt breaks up. I'll break it up sooner than I intended."

Gary stared at him in astonishment. Slowly, he shook his head. "You'll be heading for Benton to sell the pelts. I can't be going along. What good will it do to stay?"

Curdy's face was a hard mask. "The same good it will do me. I haven't been in Benton for four years. Or any American town for that matter."

80

Gary's bewilderment grew. More feeling was on Curdy's face than he had ever seen.

"I'm like you are. I have to live in the breaks. Her mother was a Cree, Gary. She died at Dawn's birth."

Gary stared at him. "She's your daughter?"

Curdy was silent a long moment before he said, "Yes."

Gary realized the memories that paraded through his mind.

"I raised her, Gary. Everything was fine until she was fourteen. She knew laughter until then. I worked fourteen years at my anvil and didn't mind it. We were making it real good. Then she caught the eye of the sheriff. Too well. He raped her."

It was simply said but the more horrible because of it. "I killed him. It wasn't hard to do. But the town didn't figure their sheriff was worth a half-Indian girl. I got out just before they came for me. I headed for the breaks. Four years, Gary. It's been a long time."

So many things were understandable now. Gary said helplessly, "My God. The kind of men you've kept her around."

The passion was raw in Curdy. "Don't you think there hasn't been a time when she hasn't been on my mind. To keep her near me I had to bring her with me. Don't you think I can see what's ahead? I haven't heard her laugh in four years. Every man in this camp knows I'd kill him if he touched her. But I've seen the way Ruch looks at her. One of these days, he'll find his moment. I'm getting afraid of going to sleep while he's around. I'd like to get him out of camp before I have to kill him."

Gary scowled at him, and it put a hurt in his bruised flesh. "What are you asking me?"

"I'm getting older and more tired. I'm asking you to help me. Ruch backed away before the two of us."

"I could be another Ruch."

Curdy shook his head. "I doubt that. Your fight with that Captain was over a woman. I figure you've got her waiting for you. That makes you different."

"Are you letting Ruch come back next year?"

"I'd kill the bastard before I let it happen. All I want to do is to get him away from us. Next year's a long time to look ahead."

Gary sighed. "I guess I owe you that much." He scowled again as he thought of another fight with Ruch. "I'll use a gun on him, if he bothers me again."

Curdy thrust out a hand, and its clasp was fervent. "Done. I've got a shack in Carroll that we've been spending the summer in. You could spend it there."

Events were shaping a course that Gary didn't want. "You mean I could be a wolfer next winter?"

"At least it'd give you something to do. A man has to have that."

Gary wanted to rave as he felt the fence drawing tighter about him.

"I know," Curdy said in understanding. "A man feels like going crazy when he doesn't see which way to turn. I'll see you in the morning."

Gary walked away. Curdy knew what he talked about. He had been walking along the road Gary was just starting on.

He swept the robe aside and stepped inside. Summers and Tindle's snoring carried to him. He found the third robe on the floor and sank down on it. What with the snoring and his hurting, he doubted if he would be able to sleep. It came much sooner than he expected.

Chapter
TEN

He awoke in the morning and moved gingerly against the aching. The first hard pounding had lessened, but he would have enough left today to be aware of it.

Summers sat up and groped for his boots. His mouth sagged as he saw Gary. "What the hell happened to you?"

He reached over and shook Tindle awake. "Look at him."

Tindle's mouth fell open. "Jesus!"

Gary kept his face blank. It was in no shape to attempt a grin. "Ruch and I had an argument last night. He was fooling around my horse."

"You whipped him?" That was disbelief in Summers' voice.

Gary didn't feel like arguing it with them. Wait until they saw Ruch. They could make their own conclusion. Maybe he was better off that he didn't have a mirror; he didn't have to look at his reflection.

Summers fired the stove and put more buffalo meat in the pot. "He won't forget it," he said as he worked. "You keep an eye on him."

Gary's answer was short. "I intend to."

He wasn't as hungry as he was last night, but the meal still tasted good. He had to chew each bite with care. His mouth hurt.

Curdy was waiting when Gary stepped out of doors. "Here's a better pistol." He handed Gary a cartridge belt and gun, and Gary was happy to strap it on.

He saw Ruch near the wagons. "Has he said anything to you about it?"

Curdy grinned. "If he knew I had a part, he didn't say anything about it."

"I might as well find out what he intends doing about it." Gary's nod to Curdy said, stay out of this.

He strode toward Ruch, and the man turned at his approach. Gary didn't know how his own face looked. But he sure as hell couldn't look any worse than Ruch did.

Ruch's face was baffled. The last thing he remembered was sitting astride and slugging away at Gary. The next thing he woke up stretched out in the snow.

Gary thought it was best that Curdy kept out of this. Ruch was a brute of a man. Gary felt differently about everything since he learned of Curdy's responsibilities.

"Ruch, I don't intend starting it all over again. But stay away from me. The next time you come after me, have a gun in your hand."

He had marked Ruch's face, and he enjoyed its vivid coloring. If Ruch got the same pleasure out of his handiwork, let him.

The ending of it had Ruch confused. Some restraint was holding him; at least, for the moment. "Don't crowd me," he growled. He wheeled away from Gary and stomped away.

Gary rejoined Curdy. "He doesn't know how it ended, and it's got him puzzled. I didn't bring you into it." He shook his head at the argument in Curdy's face. "What good would it do?"

Curdy blew out a breath. "Maybe you're right. Last night might hold him for a while." He squinted at Gary. "Are you working with us today?"

"I made that decision last night." Gary didn't know what he was going to do. He guessed he could learn.

Curdy walked with him toward the picket line. "I imagine you'll get a bellyful of it quick enough. I was planning on putting out more poisoned bait today, but we'll clean up what's down and call it an end. I guess I'm in a hurry to see it over. I don't know what keeps a man in it, unless he has to. He's cold and tired and dirty all winter long. And he faces real danger every day he's out. No man has any use for him but another wolfer, and the Indians hate us worst of all."

He nodded at the question in Gary's face. "Didn't you know that? We poison buffalo carcasses to kill wolves. Indian dogs eat strychnined bait and die, and sometimes the Indians eat the dogs. He blames his sick belly on us. But he doesn't stand much of a chance with the trade muskets most of them carry. But now and then, they catch a lone wolfer. I've seen wolfers so arrow-filled that they look like a pincushion. A man keeps his eyes open, or he doesn't last long."

Curdy finished saddling his horse. He reached for another saddle to throw on a second horse. "Dawn's," he said in brief explanation.

Sure, Gary thought. Curdy wouldn't let her stay by herself at the camp. She would have to stay near Curdy, regardless of what he did.

All the rest were mounted except for Summers. He drove the wagon that was almost empty. He waved at Gary. The gesture faded when he caught Ruch glowering at him. Ruch ignored Gary. And he wasn't looking at

Dawn. It suited Gary fine, but he didn't think it would last long. Ruch was seething inwardly, and he would chew on it until it choked him.

The subject of strychnine interested Gary, and he talked to Curdy about it as he rode.

"We won't poison any more bait this winter," Curdy said. "The wolves we'll skin are the ones left from our last poisoning. A man handles the stuff with respect. Just breathing those fumes can get you. The wolves eat the poisoned bait and go crazy trying to get to water. You can see where they've snapped up all the snow all around them."

They crested a slope, and Curdy pointed ahead of him. "There are the buffalo we shot."

Gary saw twenty buffalo carcasses dotted about on the ground. Spotted about them were the dead wolves. He would say something near a hundred dead wolves were scattered about. He looked with curiosity at the first wolf he passed. It was an old dog wolf, and he would say it was better than six feet in length without counting its brush. Its mouth was stretched in a final snarl, and the yellow eyes were set in a bitter glazing.

"Got an extra knife?" he asked Curdy. He didn't relish what lay ahead of him, but it would be better than just sitting around. He hefted the knife. It had a gleaming sharpness, and he knew better than to test its sharpness with his thumb. He had skinned a couple of wolves before, but they had been freshly killed. These had a hard night's freezing in them, and their stiffness said it was going to be a hard job.

As he started he felt eyes on him, and he turned his head. Dawn watched him; not from any friendliness, for her eyes had a sardonic gleam. He thought her attitude said she doubted he could do it.

Gary found out in a hurry how awkward and slow he was. He was doing a thorough job butchering the pelt. Its size made the carcass difficult to handle, and his face burned. The longer she watched him, the tougher it made it. He swore to himself, and the embarrassment grew in him. Some of the wolfers were already on their second wolf.

Curdy came by and looked at Gary's multilated skin. "Damn it. I better take that knife away before you ruin every hide you touch."

He wiped Gary's knife blade on his pant leg. "If you want to do something, trade places with Summers. Collect the hides and bale them."

Gary nodded sourly. Dawn still watched him, and it built up his resentment. Why had he agreed to stay here longer? He didn't want any part of a wolfer's life.

Just handling the pelts was hard work, too. He stopped the wagon beside each one and picked it up. He straightened it out and put it on a bale. When the bales reached substantial size, he roped the skins together. He soon learned why a wolfer's clothes looked as they did. Before the day was finished, his clothing was stained and smeared. A few more days of this, and nobody would be able to pick him out from the others.

He kept track and by the end of the day, he had gathered a hundred and four wolf skins. He was glad the day was over, glad to be able to get back to the crude accommodations the dugouts offered. He wiped his hands on a remaining patch of snow, then wiped them on the cleanest part of his pants he could find.

His face was blank as he drove the wagon back to camp. He didn't care what the wolfers would get from these pelts; they had earned it.

He ate more buffalo meat for the night's meal, and

his appetite wasn't as keen as it had been. He hadn't been able to wash his hands, and the smell of wolf blood seemed to fill his nostrils.

Summers offered his plug of tobacco again, and Gary shook his head. He thought of Curdy spending four winters in this business and didn't see how he stood it.

Summers rolled over on his side to face Gary. "Curdy says we're breaking camp sometime tomorrow and heading for Benton."

That was good news. Gary didn't have to offer to spend another day like this one. Some thought struck him, and he asked, "Does Curdy go with you?"

"He can't," Summers said soberly. "I'll bring back his share."

Gary frowned. Maybe he was judging wolfers only by their appearance, but he would hate to put this much trust in any of them. "Where will you find him?"

"Carroll. He's lived there the last two summers."

Gary remembered Curdy saying something about the place. Anything would be better than a wolfer's camp.

Chapter
ELEVEN

It was a big relief to see the wolfers leave for Fort Benton. The men laughed and joked as they packed their possessions. Their eagerness to leave showed plainly. Curdy's face was sober as he watched them. Gary guessed the man hurt not to be going with them. Hell, Gary thought angrily. He hurt as much as Curdy did. Dawn's face showed nothing, but then it never did.

Summers hauled up the loaded wagon before Curdy. "See you in about three weeks, Hale."

Curdy nodded. "I'll be looking for you."

Summers put the team into motion and followed the others. Curdy didn't move for several minutes. Gary thought, the longer you stand and watch them, the longer it'll hurt.

"I guess we'd better get moving," Curdy said. He was free within certain limits, but its binding was always with him. Gary knew how he felt. Wasn't he in the same position?

Ruch was the last one to put a final look on them, and Gary didn't know whether or not it was on him or Curdy. He wondered what was in the man's head. He hoped their paths wouldn't cross again.

Curdy turned toward the picket line. "I guess we might as well get saddled and packed."

The picket line looked almost deserted with only the three horses on it. Gary finished saddling and started to offer Dawn help with her saddling. She gave him a look that stopped him. How soon would he learn to never offer her anything?

They were in the saddle within fifteen minutes, and Curdy carried two rifles.

He leaned over and handed one of them to Gary. "It might come in handy," he said gruffly.

Gary examined the weapon. He had never owned a finer rifle. He threw it up in an imaginary sighting, and it came up sweetly to his shoulder. He nodded his thanks as he slipped the rifle into its boot.

Curdy headed east by north, and he rarely spoke. Gary was completely lost, but Curdy appeared to know where he was headed. The day was noticeably warm, and only an occasional patch of snow remained. A few more days like this, and the grass would jump. It made him think of his cattle and what was happening to them. Gone, he thought bleakly. The army had probably confiscated them. He forced his mind off of them. He couldn't do anything about it.

"Keep your eyes peeled," Curdy advised. "This is Indian country."

Curdy's words put tension in Gary. He would hate to run into a bunch of Indians, with only two rifles against them.

It was deadly serious with Curdy, for Gary noticed he swept the country with probing eyes from every height they climbed. The country remained empty and desolate. It was hard for man to believe that people lived in it.

They came down a slope and rode the edge of dense

forest. Gary saw the dark, huddled form the same time as Curdy said, "Dawn, hold it here."

He moved forward, Gary on his heels. He didn't need Curdy's attitude to tell him that was bad news ahead of them.

They stared down at the dead man. He was stuck with a good three dozen arrows. Whoever it was hadn't been alert enough to avoid the Indians who had found him. Gary took his eyes from the red, raw wound where the hair had been. That put a queasiness in a man's belly.

"I know him," Curdy said in a wooden voice. "Kinbad. He hunted with Dawson's bunch. It looks like he wolfed one day too long."

When Curdy looked at Kinbad, did he put himself in the man's place? It could be, Gary thought. It made it worse for Curdy, for he had Dawn with him.

Curdy swung down. "We'll pile rocks on him."

It was the best they could do for Kinbad. Gary started to agree and broke in the middle of it. Motion to his right caught his attention. Horsemen were coming at a breakneck pace, and they were close enough for Gary to identify them.

"Hale!" he yelled.

Curdy's head swung in the direction Gary was pointing, and he cursed. "Assiboines or Blackfeet. It looks like you're going to use that rifle."

He put his horse into a dead run, and Gary pounded after him. Dawn had her mount going before they passed her, but she hadn't started soon enough, and she was going to fall behind. Gary slowed enough to let her drop in between Curdy and himself.

He looked back, and he could swear they had gained

on them. This morning, he had been glad to see the wolfers leave. Now he wished they were here. He turned his head every few strides. He thought there was ten or eleven of them, and they were close enough for the shrill yippings to carry to them.

His heart lodged in his throat, and his eyes were horrified. Dawn's pony tripped and was going down, and it seemed as though it was happening in slow motion. Dawn was thrown, and Gary was by her before he could haul in Bullet. He pulled him up, and Bullet wheeled in a tight turn.

Gary ran him back, and Dawn's pony was on its hoofs and pounding on. Gary could breathe as he saw that Dawn was on her feet again.

He raced back and wheeled Bullet again. He waved frantically at her as he came on again, and she understood what he meant. She was running as he approached her, and her hands were stretched to him.

He slowed Bullet a little, and an arm was extended to her. He caught and steadied her as she made her jump, and his arm wrapped around the small of her back. He felt her hands grab him, and he pushed and steadied her behind him. Curdy must have looked back and saw what had happened. Gary motioned Curdy on, and Curdy turned again.

Gary looked back toward the Indians again, and this had cost them precious distance. The yipping had a new note of ferocity, and they would gain faster because Bullet was doubly burdened.

Curdy slowed until they were abreast of him, and his face was set. He saw what Gary did. They weren't going to be able to outrun them.

A coulee opened up ahead of them, and Gary pointed to it. He hoped Curdy understood what he meant.

He slowed Bullet and grabbed the rifle from its boot. "Jump," he yelled at Dawn.

He kicked a foot free of the stirrup and waited until she jumped. He followed her and lit running. He fought to regain his balance and thought he was going to go down, then his steps were solid.

But Dawn was down and struggling to stand. He whirled and ran back to her, reaching a hand to her. He jerked her to her feet. Her face was tight with strain, but there was no panic in it. He didn't have to ask her if she was all right, for she was running with him.

He jumped into the coulee, and she was right beside him. He turned his head to locate Curdy, and Curdy was running toward the coulee. He slithered down the bank, and his chest heaved with the hard exertion.

Gary watched Bullet and Curdy's horse gallop on away. Dawn's pony was well ahead of the other two. His eyes were bleak. It left them in a hell of a shape.

The Indians were coming hard, and the narrowing distance let Gary see the painted faces, the mouths stretched wide with their yelling. He snugged the rifle butt to his shoulder. He had never fired this rifle, and he had a big question to ask it. Did it sight and carry true?

He heard Curdy's panting beside him. "Make them count," and an unevenness pulled at his words.

Gary judged the distance. He hoped those Indians would be carrying trade muskets, short ranged against a modern, repeating rifle. He concentrated on his target, followed it for several yards and pulled the trigger.

The Indian threw up his arms. Gary was close enough to see the smashing shock mold the face and the arms went up. The Indian momentarily froze into a rigid statue. He stayed on the horse's back for a couple more strides, then toppled and fell to the ground.

Gary swung the muzzle over and picked out his next target. He fired again, and another rider was plucked from a horse's back.

Curdy whooped and fired. Gary thought the Indian was going off, then he painfully regained his balance and slewed the horse in a wide circle. The Indian was gripping hard to keep his seat, as the horse pounded away.

Gary had no time to pick out clear impressions. He leveled on another Indian, and the bullet swept the man from his mount. The action loosened Gary's tight grip of fear, and he thought of only finding another target.

"Come on, damn you," Curdy yelled, and Gary knew how he felt.

In the space of a few breaths, four Indians had been dropped, or hit, and it broke their hard desire to reach them. The forward surge was smashed, and horses wheeled in wild disarray as the Indians tried to turn out of that deadly fire. The yipping had stopped as riders drummed their heels against their horse's flanks to escape.

Curdy fired for the second time. A rider might have lurched before he galloped on.

Gary fired again and thought he missed. Those Indians were going as fast as they came.

"Goddam," Curdy said in exultation. "I thought your first couple of shots were too long. You broke them. I didn't know how well I was doing when I gave you that rifle."

Gary's heartbeat tried to return to normal. "Will they be back?"

Curdy shook his head. "I doubt it. Not with losses like that."

Gary stared after the vanishing riders. He hoped Curdy was right, but he couldn't be certain. The Indians might come back again with reinforcements. At least, he was sure they would return to pick up the fallen ones. The smartest thing they could do was to get away as fast as possible.

"We'd better go after the horses, Hale." He stared in the direction the horses had taken, and the animals were out of sight. It might take a long walk to catch up with them. He thought he could catch Bullet. He didn't know how well Dawn and Curdy could do.

She was looking at him in an odd manner, and he smiled at her. She quickly turned her head, and his smile remained. He didn't know what she thought, but he was certain those thoughts had changed.

They walked better than a mile, looking behind them with every few strides. Breathing came easier when nothing moved behind them.

Gary waved the two still as he saw Bullet a couple of hundred yards ahead of them. Bullet had stopped to graze, and Dawn's and Curdy's horses were on beyond him.

"I think I can catch up Bullet," Gary said. "Then I'll run down the other two."

Again Dawn swept his face with that strange look. He thought about it as he moved ahead. He would say she had made some new evaluation.

He slowed as he approached Bullet, speaking to him in a coaxing voice. He swore softly as Bullet threw up its head, snorted, and moved away.

"Bullet, you stand still, or I'll break your head." A damned horse wore a mule skull at times. He kept up those slow steps, the swearing inside him increasing at every move Bullet made. This was a hell of a time for the horse to get playful.

He was a yard from the reins when Bullet threw up

its head again. Gary jumped and made a grab, catching the reins. He was too relieved to carry his anger long.

He mounted, and the horizon behind him was empty. Now he had to catch up the other two and get out of here.

Bullet was faster than either of the others. He ran Curdy's horse down first and led him back. "Bring her with you," he said and set out after Dawn's pony.

He breathed freer when Dawn was mounted. "Hale, I think we'd better put some distance behind us."

Chapter
TWELVE

Carroll was a motley collection of mud and log huts. It existed because it was an important town, laying two hundred miles below Fort Benton. When the river was low, blocking boat passage to the army post, the steamers unloaded here.

"A rough town," Curdy said, and the remark was kind to the town.

Almost every structure had a man lounging before it. Gary felt a veiled scrutiny from them as they passed. He had seen the same type in Benton.

"Horse thieves and outlaws," Curdy murmured. "Living out the days, until some of the law's pressure eases. We've got a few men, trying to make a living here. The wood choppers supply fuel for the steamers." He smiled faintly. "The only other honest men here are the wolfers."

Gary's face was set as he scanned the town. Most of the huts had its souring garbage heap, covered with the first swarms of flies. The warming weather had brought them out, and they rose in angry, buzzing clouds as the horses passed the garbage piles. Animal offal, hides, and heads fouled the air with a stench of rotting flesh. The inhabitants were too lazy, or too indifferent to bury, or drag away the refuse.

"God," he exploded. "How does a man live like this?"

That was no mirth in Curdy's laugh. "Any way they can. Drinking whiskey when they get their hands on it. Playing cards when they have the money. The rest of the time just waiting."

Gary shook his head. This was the existence he had ahead of him.

"They mind their own business, Gary."

Was that a warning in Curdy's words? Gary thought about it. He had no intention of having anything in common with them. Maybe Curdy wasn't entirely right about these men minding their own business. Curdy surely couldn't have missed it by the way their eyes had swept over Dawn.

He was filled with anger. From the way it looked to Gary it might not be better off for Curdy and Dawn here, than it had been in the wolfer's camp.

Dawn rode ahead of them, and Curdy lowered his voice. "Don't you think I'm not aware of it. Every summer we've spent here, it gets worse."

The prospects could drive Curdy crazy, Gary admitted. He intended upon helping Curdy all he could, but how long did the man think he would stay around this town. How many empty days could he stand? It might be better to cross the river and go on into Canada. The law there wouldn't want him, and it might be better to make a new start. He was in no rush to go into it. He would think about it.

"Stores here?" he asked.

"One. If it can be called that. It never has stocked what a man wants, or is freshly out of it."

Gary sighed. "I need about everything." Worse, he had no money. Maybe he would have to join a wood-chopping gang until he earned a few dollars.

Curdy glanced at him. "That last hut up ahead is ours. Dawn tried to keep it up to a certain standard."

A crusty grin creased his face. "She raises hell, if I bet too careless."

Gary looked at her. There had been a subtle change in her since they had driven off the Indians. Not anything that he could put a finger on, but it was there. She still didn't do much talking, but she didn't ignore him as she had formerly done.

Curdy's words put the problem of lodging in Gary's mind. He couldn't expect to live with Dawn and her father.

Curdy guessed at what troubled him. "Shelter here doesn't make a man too much of a problem. Always three or four empty huts in town. Some of the builders just go off and never come back, and nobody hears what happened to them. Others might get shot when they go into town, or slapped into jail. This population has a pretty constant turnover."

Gary nodded. He wished all of his problems were solved as easily as shelter. He had to keep constant control upon the wildness that was with him, or it would rise up and engulf him.

Dawn had the hut's door open and was inside by the time Curdy and Gary reached it. The floor was littered, the debris of a winter's living by small animals that had found entrance. If the cracks between the planking flooring weren't big enough, they simply gnawed them a larger one. Gary would say a pack rat had built busily in a far corner. The absent months had piled up dust upon everything.

Curdy sighed. "I know that look on her face. She takes a pride in the way this place looks. We'd better get ready to work."

The remaining hours of the day were busy enough for Gary. Dawn swept up the accumulated dust and debrise, and Gary carried it out in old buckets to empty them. Every time he approached the back door to enter it, he glanced up at the roof. Curdy wasn't fooling anybody, trying to make them believe it took this long to inspect the roof. Gary grinned. Curdy better give him special treatment, or he would say something to Dawn that would send her out in a hurry.

The floor was clean, and the smell of dust inside the hut was beginning to fade. He picked up a chair, that needed some repairing, and carried it outside.

He was surprised to see that the sun was westering fast. The work had made the hours go fast. A man made those hours move by in a hurry, if he had something to keep him occupied. It was a knowledge that he had learned long ago.

Curdy scrambled off the roof. "Roof's in good shape."

"It ought to be. You spent enough time up there to build a new one."

Curdy chuckled. "She'll be on me before too long. I never get by with much from her."

He looked inside the house. "I thought she'd have supper started. Where did she go?"

Gary shook his head as he drove another nail. "She didn't say anything to me."

He thought of those glances resting on her as they had ridden into town. "Where did you think she went?"

"The store, I guess." Something in Gary's face put strain in Curdy. "Hell, she always has."

"It's another year," Gary said curtly. He stepped inside and buckled on his gun belt.

He checked Curdy's movement. "I can handle it. I'm

only going down to the store to help her carry the stuff back."

He gave Curdy a reassuring look as he passed him. He hoped it was no more than that.

He approached the store, and she was backed up against the rickety porch railing. Both of her arms were burdened, and every time she tried to move, one or the other of two men blocked her passage.

"Aw come on, Dawn," one of them said. "How come you're so unfriendly this year?"

She started to answer and stopped when she saw Gary. Her face relaxed.

"Let her pass," Gary said evenly.

The pair turned to face him, and their eyes narrowed. They were small, thin men with worn clothes and boots that had seen too much use. One of them wore a black, sweeping mustache, and both had a razor sharpness in their faces.

"Hell, Mister," one of them said. "We were only offering to carry her stuff."

"She didn't ask it." Gary's eyes swept from face to face. "I won't say it again."

They spent a long moment evaluating him, and Gary tensed.

"Any way you want it. Fists or guns."

They saw the readiness in him, for one of them said, "Hell! We were just being friendly." Both of them whipped around and walked into the store.

Gary held out his arms for her packages, and her eyes rested on his face. She looked down as she breathed, "Thank you."

He thought her 'thank you' came easier than the first time, but he didn't press it. He slowed and shortened his stride to match hers.

"You don't have to let them bother you again."

She nodded, and her expression was lighter. He thought, she's had too many bad times already.

Curdy raved when Dawn told him about it. "They were only teasing me, Pa. They left when Gary told them to. Forget it."

Curdy wasn't ready to drop it. Gary watched them both. Dawn scurried from table to stove, wanting to get the supper on. She's known too much violence, Gary thought. He felt sorry as he wondered, if she would ever escape it.

"Who were they?" Curdy demanded.

"Lee and Ord." Her voice was low. "They never bothered me before."

They hadn't, Gary thought. But then she was a year older.

She ate with her eyes downcast, and the blackness didn't entirely leave Curdy's face.

Gary ate with full appetite. She was a good cook. He tried to keep the conversation going, and it stumbled along. He felt pity for both. They were familiar with a fear, and it stayed with them.

Chapter
THIRTEEN

Curdy loaned him a couple of blankets, and Gary slept in the closest empty hut. It was dirty, and the smell of undisturbed dust filled his nose. Sleep wouldn't come readily to him, and he thought about many things. Dawn's face kept appearing before him. Too many things happened to people that they couldn't do anything about. He thought about his former life and of the plans he had. He turned restlessly. In one breath of time all that had been changed. He tried to recall Elizabeth's face, and it stayed hazy.

The wildness was surging up in him again. How could he stop thinking about it? What did a man do about something he couldn't help? He fell asleep without determining what he was going to do.

Dawn awakened him by announcing that breakfast was ready. She stood in the doorway of his hut, and that could be a slight flush in her face as he looked up at her. He remembered the first time he had seen her and contrasted the difference in her. "I'll be over in a few minutes," he said.

He dressed, hating to put back on the dirty clothes, and he couldn't do much about it. He walked over to Curdy's house, and he picked up the smell of good cooking as he stepped inside. The chairs were placed around the table, and for a moment the sight built the illusion of contentment. The trouble was that he couldn't keep the barrier, against what was outside, up for long.

Curdy had shaved this morning, and Gary rubbed his thumb across his beard. "That's what I should be doing." He added with wry humor, "My razor's a long way off."

"We'll go down to the store," Curdy said. "He might have one. And he should have something in the way of clothes."

Gary felt the burn in his face. It went against a man's grain to say that he didn't have a penny in his pockets.

Curdy guessed at his embarrassment. "Are you too proud to accept a loan for right now?"

The stiffness faded in Gary. "I guess I could do that. But I haven't got any idea when I can repay it."

Curdy grinned. "You let me worry about that."

He looked back from the door. "Dawn, stay here until we get back."

His face was sober. The restrictions he had to put on Dawn weren't pleasant.

Jenkins looked up from behind the counter of his store as they came into it. He was a sour, tired-looking man, and his outlook had cut permanent, sagging lines in his face. He was a slat-thin man with stooped shoulders. If Gary had to live long in Carroll, he would look like Jenkins.

Curdy introduced Gary, and Jenkins acknowledged it. "Hale, this damned winter just about took me off."

What kept Jenkins here? Gary wasn't curious enough to ask questions. He doubted that any wise man asked questions here.

Curdy asked for a razor, and Jenkins frowned. "I had a couple sent in a few years back. I sold one of them. I can't remember when I saw the last one."

104

"Look for it." Curdy turned to Gary as Jenkins disappeared into the back room. "You can always borrow mine."

Gary could do that, but a man couldn't go too long or far without a few possessions of his own.

Jenkins had a small, oblong box when he came back. The small triumph of finding the razor hadn't alleviated the sourness of his face.

Looking at the razor put an itching in Gary's beard. He wanted to be getting the beard off.

He spent twenty dollars before he was through, and Curdy haggled over the price of every item. Gary learned that the first price Jenkins stated was the only one he hoped to get.

Gary bought two pair of jeans, two shirts and several pairs of socks. His hat and boots were still good. He finished out his buying with a razor strop, towels and soap. He topped off the growing pile with a half dozen sacks of cigarette makings.

"That everything?" Curdy asked.

"This sets me up good," Gary answered gruffly. "I don't even begin to know where it will come from."

Curdy grinned. "You made a good day for Jenkins."

"You come back," Jenkins said. His voice hadn't lightened much.

Curdy took some of the items to carry and turned to the door with Gary. As they came to it, a man came through it.

"Munn," Curdy said, and it was a restrained greeting.

Munn nodded. "Hale." His eyes swept over Gary in a brief appraisal. His face was hawk-sharp, the cheeks hollowed under high bones. His mouth was a harsh slash, and Gary read a hard competence in him.

"Munn, this is Gary Hobart."

Gary took the hand offered him. He asked no questions of Munn, and Munn asked nothing from him.

"Lew and Ord around?" Curdy asked.

"See them earlier this morning, Hale. You don't have to give them any warnings. They told me about funning Dawn yesterday."

Again, those eyes made their weighing of Gary. "It won't happen again."

"I appreciate that, Munn." Curdy stepped by him, and Gary followed.

"That's a hard customer," Gary said when they got outside. "I've heard he has a long record."

"He has, Gary. He kind of stands on the top of the heap around here. We got along well enough before." His eyes crinkled in humor. "He must have seen something in you. I'm glad it's that way."

Gary's eyes were thoughtful. He hoped it was. Maybe Curdy could lift some of the girl's restrictions.

Curdy pointed out the directions of a small stream, a half mile out of town. The deepest hole Gary found in it was only waist deep, cold enough to chatter his teeth. He stayed in until he was clean, then dried himself with a rough, husk towel. He felt a hundred percent better after he had dressed in the new clothes. He almost left the old clothes where he had dropped them, then picked them up, his eyes dubious. He didn't know what could be done about getting them cleaned.

He found Curdy just coming out of his hut. At Gary's question, he jerked his head. "She's over at your place."

Gary's face didn't lighten as he approached it. The phrase "your place" carried no balm, for it didn't mean a thing to him. It replaced nothing for him, and at least, it was a sorry substitution.

Dawn was inside, mopping the floor. He watched her for a moment. She was an attractive woman, and he wondered what life would turn out for her. His presence touched her, and she turned her head.

He frowned. "You don't have to do that."

Her face fell at some note in his tone, and he erased the frown. Maybe what she was doing was an attempt to repay what she considered she owed. Certainly, she tried to make things more bearable, but it didn't eliminate or make the past more bearable. He recognized the mood he was in this morning, but he could do nothing to get rid of it.

He dropped the old clothes on the floor. "I don't know if anything can be done with it. I'll be back before evening."

He wanted to saddle up Bullet and put some ground behind him. The brooding had him in a firm grip. Maybe riding would let it escape.

He rode every day for the next two weeks, aimless wandering, and he knew why. This waiting for the days to pass without some purpose was driving him crazy.

He did the hunting when they needed a deer, but how many could they use? His appetite for venison, the last time he had eaten it, had been slim. He would give a lot to have a big slab of beefsteak, and the longing for everything he had known was more poignant than ever. His mood reflected on Dawn and Curdy. The girl had retreated behind that earlier wall, answering with as few words as she could. Curdy was almost as reticent, and he watched Gary with veiled eyes. Both of them acted as though everything was Gary's fault, and it irritated him.

The day was slipping away when Gary turned Bullet toward the little pocket of grass, a quarter-mile behind

107

Curdy's house. Hobbling the horses kept them from straying, and the pond, formed by the spring, furnished ample water.

Curdy's and Dawn's animals were there, Curdy's at the far end, Dawn's drinking at the pond. Gary hadn't asked either of them to ride with him. How could he explain to them that he wanted to be alone?

He saw a tawny flash in the big oak limbs some ten yards from the water's edge. He had to catch another sign of the animal to identify it. It worked its way closer, and it was a big mountain lion. Its muscles were tensing for the spring at the pony, and it was ready to make it.

Gary jerked the rifle from its scabbard. It had to be a snap shot, letting instinct take the place of timing his aim. He pulled, and there was a lot in the shock to the animal. He scored while it was in mid-air, and he saw the arc of the spring broken. But the lion still had enough left to come close enough, for a raking forepaw ripped at the pony's rump.

The pony threw up its head and bugled in wild terror. It jumped straight forward into the water, and its hoofs slashed for more momentum. The threshing steps carried it forward, but they also buried it deeper. When it could no longer move, it was bogged down half way up to its barrel. Its eyes rolled wildly, and it whipped its head about. But it was held fast.

Gary thanked the habit of carrying a rope with him. He built his loop and made his cast. The loop settled over the pony's head and tightened about its neck. Bullet was a good roping animal, and Gary tightened up the slack.

The rope hummed under the strain. He asked for all the power Bullet had, but it wasn't enough. The pony's hoofs didn't give a bit.

He stopped Bullet and set him forward, putting slack

into the rope. He loosened the dally and let the rope fall. If the pony was coming out, somebody had to go in and free the animal's hoofs.

He whirled Bullet around and raced back toward the hut. He was yelling before he reached it. Curdy and Dawn came out, their faces asking what the yelling was about.

"Dawn's pony is mired down in the pond," Gary said. He turned Bullet and waited for them to reach him. Her face was agonized, and he helped her behind him. Curdy would have to pound along behind them.

"A mountain lion," he said to her. "The pony jumped into the pond and stuck."

Her face worked with hatred as she looked at the lion. Its eyes were glazed in death. She looked back at her pony, and the agony was back on it.

Curdy was blowing down when he reached them. It took only a few words to make him understand what had happened.

"You take Bullet, Hale," Gary said. "I'll see if I can free the pony's hoofs before you put strain on the rope."

Curdy nodded and climbed into the saddle. Gary handed him the end of the rope. He waded into the pond, and the water still had a chill to it.

He had to put his face under the water to reach the hoofs. He clawed big handfuls of mud and straightened to breathe while he threw it from him. It took a dozen handfuls before he thought its clinging was weakened.

"Try it, Hale."

He watched the rope grow taut, and he twisted on the animal's tail, trying to lift it out of the mud. It was going to take more digging, and he waved Curdy to slack off. It took fifteen minutes of more gasping labor before he saw the pony start under the rope's hauling.

"Keep on, keep," he yelled.

Once the pony's momentum started, it built, and it came out with a rush. Curdy slackened the rope once the pony's hoofs were out on firm ground.

Dawn was the first to reach her pony. Her eyes were distressed as she saw the oozing of red streaks from that lion's raking paw.

Gary examined the wound. It was bleeding fairly free, but he didn't find muscle damage.

"We'll get back to the hut and put some of that salve you used on me." He wanted to get the distress from her face. "She'll be all right."

He let Curdy stay in the saddle and walked with Dawn, leading the pony by the rope. There wasn't any sense in him muddying his saddle.

The pony trembled under the medication he smeared on her rump. "I don't think she'll even be stiff from it."

Dawn drew a deep breath. "If you hadn't been along at the right time—"

He grinned to take the worry from her. "But I was."

A smile started at her lip corners, weak at first, but steadily strengthening. Then her laughter came.

He didn't understand it at first, and he thought it was directed at him. "What's funny?" he demanded.

She choked off her mirth. "I was just thinking of how hard you are on new clothes."

He looked at his muddy clothes, and a wry grin came back to him. "I hope it doesn't happen this often."

He could get out of the wet, muddy clothes, but he had to wait on his boots to dry. His eyes were troubled. In a short time, he had been thrown into contact with her a lot. He had been able to do several things for her, and he wasn't sure that he wanted to.

Chapter
FOURTEEN

Summers arrived that evening. His yelling outside came in the middle of supper, and Curdy's eyes shone with pleasure.

"I've been expecting him any day now," he said, pushing to his feet.

Dawn and Gary followed him outside. Curdy pulled Summers from his horse and mauled him in greeting.

"Wait a minute," Summers wailed. "Wait until I tell you I lost all of your money in Benton."

His laugh boomed out at the fleeting expression on Curdy's face. "Wait until you see what I brought back with me."

Gary shook his hand, and Dawn greeted him. Did she have a special feeling for the man, or had her wariness softened the last few days? Gary didn't know.

Curdy hustled Summers inside, and Dawn filled a plate for him. Summers talked between mouthfuls.

"Everything went right for me in Benton. Hale, I got two dollars and a half for pelts."

Gary didn't see as much joy in Curdy's face as he expected, then he realized a big sum of money meant nothing here. The things, for him to buy, simply just didn't exist. He wondered what Curdy did with his money. He could see nothing for it but burying.

"What else good happened to you?" Curdy asked.

"I cleaned out every game in Benton. Every card I touched couldn't turn wrong." Summers' laugh rang out again. "I've got every pocket loaded.

"What are you going to do with it?" Curdy grunted.

"Hell, I'm going to clean out, Carroll. I won't leave a dollar in it."

Curdy's face was cynical. "Good luck. There's some pretty slick card players in town."

His face changed with some thought, and he expressed it. "Did you see Ruch after you got to Benton?"

Summers' look sobered. "Several times. I stayed away from him as much as I could. Every time I saw him, he was drunk."

Dawn was clearing off the table, and Summers waited until she moved away. He lowered his voice. "He had only one thing in his head. Getting even with you two. He said he was coming to Carroll."

Gary looked at Curdy, and Curdy looked grim. "What did he do?"

Summers shrugged. "He was still in Benton when I left. He always had a big mouth."

Curdy's eyes burned. "Maybe it isn't just talk this time. Finish your coffee, Summers. I want to talk to Gary."

He moved to the door, and Gary followed him. He looked back, and Dawn had a question on her face.

"What do you think, Gary?" Curdy rolled a cigarette and handed the makings to Gary.

Gary didn't know. "I'm one of the two who's in his head. Who's the other? You or Dawn?"

Curdy's cursing rumbled in his throat. "Goddam him. If he comes here, I'll plug him. If he even touches Dawn, she'll knife him."

Gary had seen the sheathed knife she always carried.

112

But it wasn't enough protection; not with Ruch's tremendous strength.

"I'll spend some time looking after her, Hale."

Curdy breathed a gusty sigh. "That eases my mind, Gary. Both of us will keep an eye on her. Summers will give us a hand, too."

He stared broodingly ahead of him. The worry would stay with him until Ruch's whereabouts was known. Gary understood it full well. It wasn't impossible for a man to slip in and out of Carroll. Dawn could be the answer to a man's obsession.

Whenever Dawn took a step, Gary was her shadow. The few times he wasn't near her, Curdy or Summers was. The passing days bore heavily on him. The waiting, not knowing what or when it might come, chafed him. On several occasions, he had the feeling that eyes watched him. He put that down to the product of nerves. But several times, he had given in to it, and he had seen nothing.

Dawn was going out to see the pony again, and Gary kept well behind her. He wished irritably that she didn't feel it necessary to go out here so often, but he couldn't demand that she stay fastened up in the hut.

The path, ahead of him, bent around a small, sheer bluff, and Dawn was momentarily cut out of sight. He quickened his pace.

He came around the bluff, and something blocked his swallowing. Ruch had one arm wrapped around her, and the other was plastered across her mouth. His grin turned his face evil.

"Try for the gun," Ruch said. "And I'll snap her neck."

Gary knew too well the tremendous strength Ruch

had. He could easily do what he said. He held her before him, and Gary considered his choice. He didn't dare risk a shot; the target was small enough, with her acting as a shield.

"Drop the gunbelt," Ruch ordered. His face twisted at Gary's indecision. "Goddam you! Do you want me to show you what I can do to her?"

Gary unbuckled the belt and let it drop to the ground. He was sure now what Ruch wanted. Even if he had Dawn in his mind, he wouldn't leave without a meeting with Gary. The earlier fight with him was like a thorn, festering in his head. He acted as though he knew the ground well; he had picked this spot for some reason.

Ruch released her and stepped forward.

"Get away from here, Dawn," Gary said. He had had a taste of this man before, and he didn't relish the tasting of it again. He would have to fight him the same way. This time he had to be certain he whittled away until all of Ruch's strength was gone. He wouldn't make another mistake.

Ruch came with a bull rush, and Gary sidestepped him. He planted a fist on Ruch's cheek, and it drew an angered roar.

Gary waited for him to come to him again. Dawn hadn't moved, and her eyes were wide in terror.

"Get away from here, Dawn," he repeated. If something went wrong, he didn't want her to be here.

He danced away from Ruch's charge, slugging him on the ear. Those blows had sting in them, but they didn't do nearly enough damage. He wished he had a club.

Ruch stopped the hard rushes and stalked Gary with dogged steps. Gary backed before him. The pace mounted up in a hurry and pulled panting effort out of him. When he saw his chance, he flicked in a blow.

He saw blood come out and trickle into the beard, and the number of them was making his fists sore. He caught one in the chest before he got away, and there was a numbness where the fist had landed. The man's brute power was appalling, and it was a good thing the blow hadn't landed higher on the throat. He would be down, gasping for breath.

He knew vaguely that Dawn was still here, and he couldn't waste more breath on her. A doubt began to creep up on him. His legs were getting heavy. Could he keep enough strength in them when he needed it to move away fast?

He was almost pinned against the face of the bluff, and he saw why Ruch had picked this place. The bluff would keep one direction of his retreat closed. Gary wished Dawn had listened to him; he wished she had gone and got Curdy and Summers. His breath slogged in his throat, and fire was in his lungs.

He remembered how his other fight with Ruch was going until Curdy had intervened. He needed Curdy again, and there was no humor in the thought.

He was almost pinned again, and those legs didn't carry him away as fast as he wanted them to. He wanted to yell at Ruch; hadn't he felt anything at all yet?

Ruch kept him moving backwards, and Gary felt something brush against his back, knowing it was the bluff again. He feinted one way, then tried to slip in the other, and Ruch anticipated it correctly. A hand tightened on Gary's arm, and Gary hammered away at the other. He got in a half-dozen blows, and the blood splattering from Ruch's face speckled Gary.

Ruch pulled him in close, and both arms were about him. The strength of the man was terrifying, and Gary couldn't break the grip. Ruch's roaring was a constant sound in his ears, and black specks danced before his eyes.

When he thought a total blackness would engulf him, Ruch let go of him. Gary couldn't plainly see him, and his mouth was open in frantic gasps for air. A blow smashed him in the face, and he didn't see it coming. He fell hard, and the ground smashed at him. A tiny remnant of thought remained in his head. He couldn't whip this man. He hoped Dawn had enough sense to run.

Something smashed into his ribs, sending searing agony throughout him. It came again, and he thought Ruch would kick him to pieces. Then Ruch's weight dropped onto his chest, and thumbs sought the hollow in his throat. Thumbs cut off his air, and he couldn't see.

He felt something press into his palm, and it took effect to think about it. It took too much endeavor, and his senses were fading. Then it came to him; Dawn had put the haft of her knife in his hand.

He gripped it with the remaining strength he had and swung his arm. He felt the resistance meet the knife's blade, and he drove it as far as he could. He didn't think he could pull it out, but he made it. He drove it in another arc, and that was the last he remembered.

Chapter
FIFTEEN

He thought he was unconscious, but he heard voices, and the pain kept ripping at him. It concentrated in his side and throat, and its tentacles ran all throughout him. The voices came to him from far away, and he tried to think about them. Was that Ruch? But no, he thought he heard more than one voice.

"Gary, can you stand?"

It took hard effort to make sense out of those words. It wasn't Ruch; Ruch wouldn't want him to get up.

A wet cloth touched his face, and it was a tide sweeping against the blackness that wanted to hold him. He didn't want fully to come back to consciousness; it hurt too much.

He could see three faces bending over him, and it was difficult to make them out in the hazy blur. He had to concentrate to identify them. Dawn was trying to clean his face with a wet cloth. Curdy and Summers were beside her.

"Can you hear me, Gary?"

Gary heard Curdy plainly enough, though he had to think about it. All of the faces were concerned, and Dawn looked as though she had been crying. That was hard to understand.

"I hear you, Hale." His voice didn't sound the same, and it hurt to force the words out of his throat. Things were slowly coming back to him. Where was Ruch?

"Ruch?" he croaked.

"Dead, Gary. Don't you remember?" Curdy asked. "Dawn came after us. We found you just coming to. Can you walk?"

Little bits were falling into place, and Gary recalled the finish. Dawn must have put the knife in his hand. He remembered trying to drive it through Ruch.

"I think so," he said in that rasping voice.

It took several efforts to overcome the pain that tried to keep him off of his feet. He made it with Curdy's and Summers' help, and the sheets of pain locked his teeth hard. He could make it by leaning heavily on their shoulders, and he didn't try to look at Ruch. He had taken a terrible mauling in the last few seconds of that fight. He hoped Ruch died hard.

"He damned near got me, Hale." Talking tore at his throat. "If it hadn't been for Dawn—" The rest of it was too hard to say, and he let it go.

That walk to the hut was the longest, most painful he had ever taken. He breathed hard by the time he reached it, and his legs insisted upon buckling with every step. He was bathed in sweat, and he felt feverishly hot. He didn't remember them helping him get into bed. The blackness danced around just a little beyond his vision, and he wanted to slip into it and get rid of the hurt.

He thought he had lost his sight when he came to, and he almost yelled against it. Then he saw the small light the lamp made on the table. It was night, and he had been out for a long time.

She was at his side before he could even think of cry-

118

ing out, and Curdy followed her, carrying the lamp. "Feeling any better?" he asked.

Gary grimaced. He was clear-headed, and he felt like hell. He saw the livid bruise on Dawn's cheek, and he didn't know how that had happened.

"Is she hurt?" It still rasped to talk.

Curdy shook his head. "You don't know everything that happened?"

Gary frowned at him. He didn't know, or he wouldn't ask.

"She tried to knife him, Gary. He swept her away with a swipe of his hand that flattened her. He damned near knocked her out. She crawled back and put the knife in your hand. I guess it was just about in time."

Gary stared intently at her. He saw things that he hadn't noticed before, the soft depth of her eyes, the beauty in her face. The name, Elizabeth, slipped into his mind, and he couldn't see her face at all.

He reached out and caught Dawn's hand. "I'd say we're even," he whispered.

He thought that was a rosy glow stealing into her face, but he wasn't sure. "Did I see three of you out there?" he asked.

"Dawn came for Summers and me. I never saw more worry in her." Curdy chuckled. "We couldn't get there fast enough. We had trouble bringing you back here. Ruch worked you over good. I think he broke your ribs. I wrapped them up the best I could. Your voice shows how much pressure he put on your throat. But he didn't do any permanent damage. Give you a few days, and you'll be around again."

Gary nodded weakly. He hadn't stopped staring at her. Something picked at him, and it wouldn't quite

119

come to light. Whatever she felt, showed in her face. He was so damned drained and weakened, and all he wanted to do was to go to sleep. Maybe he could think about it later.

He didn't know he still held her hand when his eyes closed. He didn't feel her gently tug it free.

It was daylight when he awakened, and stirred unwisely, for it rolled the fiery waves through him. He must be better, for he was keenly aware of every throb. He scowled at the bandaging Curdy had put around him. He was wrapped up like a cocoon. It would be some time before he made any abrupt, unwise moves. Those ribs swore at him with the slightest move.

Dawn brought him breakfast, a gruel that was thinned to almost liquid. With slow, cautious sips to protect his bruised throat, he could handle that and some coffee. He felt exhausted when he finished, and he wanted to sleep again. His eyes closed as he thought about Dawn again. Something was so different about her, something that kept hitting him with a hard awareness.

At the end of three days he insisted upon trying to stand though Dawn protested against it. He winced at the stabs that tore through him, but he could make it. He braced himself against the weakness and smiled at her.

"A man couldn't want a better nurse, Dawn."

The rosy color was back in her face, and she wouldn't meet his eyes. The bruise was fading from her face, though it was drawn. He suspected she hadn't slept much last night.

The discovery he had been hunting hit him hard. He felt more than just gratitude. He wished she would look at him; he wanted to learn more about that discovery.

"Dawn, look at me."

Slowly, she turned her face toward him. His eyes probed deep, and the color in her cheeks increased. "You know what you did for me?"

She shrugged and tried to make light of it. "Look at everything that you did for me."

He couldn't keep her attention captured, or else it was only pretense on her part. "I think I could be falling in love with you."

Her eyes came back to him, and that was a gasp in her voice. The statement had jarred her, and he had the feeling she wanted to run. Maybe he was too abrupt in his words. Maybe she needed more time to slowly approach it.

He would not press her harder, and he waited. Not too long ago he had thought himself in love with another girl. He tried to think of her, and Elizabeth's face was shadowy and without definite detail. His heart picked up tempo as he waited for Dawn to answer. Did she feel anything about him?

Her eyes were still startled, then a new emotion replaced it. "I remember how I felt when I thought he was killing you," she said brokenly.

"Dawn," he said hoarsely and held out his arms to her. She came into them, and he kissed her. Her lips seemed to have a tremulous touch that contained some old terror. Then it was all gone, and her lips firmed. He was lost in the contact, and this was something he had never known before. He didn't know how it lasted, but it told a man everything he wanted to know.

An outraged voice came from the door. "Why, goddam you! I'll kill you for this."

Curdy stomped into the room, followed by Summers.

Summers showed the same anger. Curdy's face was in an excess of rage. "I'll kill you for this."

"You won't!" Dawn cried, and her eyes blazed.

Curdy stared at her, his mouth sagging. "Are you in love with him?"

Gary answered for her. "She is, Hale. We both just found out about it. I was going to ask her to marry me before you interrupted." He felt a sick dismay at the words. How could he ask her that, with no money in his pockets, or any prospects in the future of getting it.

Curdy looked from his daughter to Gary, and his expression showed how stricken he was.

"Is that what you want, Dawn?" He sighed at her firm nod. "Then I guess you're old enough to know your own mind."

"Maybe we better congratulate him, Hale." Summers thrust out his hand. Curdy shook it next, though Gary thought there was reluctance in it. He didn't blame the doubts that must be hitting Curdy. But Gary could make a living for her. He could always join Curdy for the next winter's wolfing, though he would hate to turn to that. That was another thing to think about in the future. He had so many things to put into order.

"I was playing cards last night," Summers said. "Gary, a soldier boy was in the game. He's played the last couple of nights."

Gary felt the constriction of his heart. He didn't think the army dared come into the breaks. Maybe the soldier had come in to locate him. Maybe he would be again on the run once more.

"Did you know him?"

Summers shook his head. "They called him Mahoney. I think he's a deserter. He only had the coat part of his uniform. Maybe you'd better look over him and find out about him."

The name picked at Gary, but he couldn't place it. "Yes," he said grimly. He would check tonight. He wanted to know why that soldier was here.

Chapter
SIXTEEN

Dawn argued with Gary about him going out this night. Gary grinned at her indignation. She had a new power, and she used it.

"It won't hurt me to walk down and see about him, Dawn. I've got to know who he is." One man wasn't a great threat to him. But if this Mahoney went back to the Army and reported that he was here, then there was real danger to him.

Curdy sided with Gary. "I'm going with him, Dawn. I don't blame him wanting to know who that man is."

That stilled her, but her face was unhappy about it. "You'll be careful, won't you?"

He traced her jawline with a finger. "Even with the steps I have to take." He would have to watch them. Any carelessness would cost him a stab of pain from the healing ribs.

She didn't say another word as she watched him strap on the gunbelt, but her eyes were troubled. She understood he had to do it, but she didn't approve of it.

"You want to lean on me?" Curdy asked as they started out.

Gary grunted his "no." Mahoney! He had tried to recall the name ever since he had heard it. Maybe it would return to him after he had seen the man.

The game was held in the store, and Curdy and Gary watched it from outside the window. Mahoney was facing them, and the light was strong on him.

"I don't know him," Curdy said. "But that doesn't mean anything. I wouldn't know most of them."

"I know him." Seeing him had placed Mahoney for Gary. This was the man who had been on sentry duty at the main gate the night of the ball. Excitement was beginning to run strongly. He would never forget any part of the evening. "Blakely ripped into him. Mahoney couldn't say anything, but it was in his face. He hated Blakely's guts."

"Maybe he is a deserter, Hale. This would be a safe place for one of them to be. Do you think he's tied in with Blakely?"

"I don't know." Gary's answer was slow. Did some guilt mount in Mahoney until he ran under it? Gary wished he knew a lot of answers. "I'm ready to go back."

"What are you going to do?"

Gary didn't know, but there was a ray of hope in him.

Summers chuckled as he raked in another pot. This was the third in a row, and his luck was still running strong. It had been that way the last three nights. Mahoney's face showed distress. His loss was hurting him.

Munn gathered the cards and shuffled them. Lew and Ord and another man, called Pike, were in the game. Their faces showed the intentness of the loser.

Summers glanced around at them, and his eyes danced. He had been indiscriminate with his nicking. All of these men were in his pockets. He hoped their supply of money held out.

"Deal, Munn," he said.——

Shortly before midnight, Summers broke Mahoney. Mahoney's cursing was savage, but he made it careful not to put it on Summers.

"That breaks me," Mahoney said sullenly. He looked at Summers with glittering eyes. The chips were stacked high before him.

Summers stacked more chips. "I hate to lose you. You get some more money and come back."

Mahoney swept him with a burning glance, then turned and plunged toward the door.

"He looks like he hurts," Summers observed.

Munn shook his head. "He's not the only one." He grinned wryly. "Hell, you're going to put us back to work before we want to go."

The other three nodded their agreement.

Mahoney walked down the street, cursing Summers with every step. He was broke, and what was he going to do now? He transferred some of the blame onto himself. Why had he gotten in that game? He had had enough money to carry him into Canada, and he wanted to put more distance between him and Colonel Stenton. Stenton hadn't made an accusation, but he seemed to study Mahoney with new intensity. Did Stenton have some information that Mahoney didn't know about? Thinking about it had driven Mahoney crazy. A week of the pressure had made up his mind. He would desert. He hated the damned Army anyway.

He had waited until after payday, and he had rifled the pockets of his barrack companions while they were under heavy sleep. He was a long way from the post by the time the next day had dawned. That had been a long, hard ride, but he hadn't seen a man until he reached Carroll.

He cursed again as he thought of the stacks of chips piled up before Summers. Why did the man's damned luck hold up that long? What he could do with the money Summers had.

He stopped, and his breathing quickened as the thought struck him. He could take that money away from Summers, if he went home alone. He thought that Summers had taken this way the other nights. He could wait here behind the tree, stepping out as Summers went by it.

His heart beat faster as he went over all phases of it. He thought of clubbing Summers with a gun barrel, but what if the blow wasn't hard enough, and Summers got a yell out? It was close enough to the store to carry that far. He touched the knife in its sheath at his belt. No, this was better; it was the deadliest, silent thing he could use.

He settled down to his waiting. If the other three came out with Summers, he would have to forget it for tonight. The waiting honed him fine, and he swore under his breath.

He saw a figure come out of the store's door and turn this way. It passed through the light washing from the window, and Mahoney plainly saw it.

His breathing was a low, soft sigh. The waiting was over.

The knife was in his hand as he stepped out behind Summers. He made not a sound; even his breathing was slow and shallow. Summers didn't suspect a thing.

An arm clamped around his throat, and every sound was blocked in Summers. He couldn't yell out, but he could struggle. His arms threshed about, and his body jerked as he tried to throw Mahoney off. But that was only for the briefest of seconds before the knife plunged into his back. His body went rigid, then his weight slumped against Mahoney's arm.

He looked about him, and he saw nothing that could disturb him. That had been a good thrust, and not a sound had called attention to him.

He dragged Summers to a shallow ditch a few yards behind the tree and withdrew the knife. He looked about him again and was satisfied. He wiped the blade on Summers' pants and started rifling his pockets. My God, the man had all of them loaded.

Gary awakened in the morning and frowned at the other bed. Summers had been sleeping with him, since he had arrived, and he hadn't come in at all last night. Gary was a fairly light sleeper, and he hadn't missed hearing him the other nights.

The frown remained on his face as he dressed. Summers had probably spent a riotous night that had used it all, but just the same, Gary wanted to know where he has. He thought he had better tell Curdy about this.

He beckoned Curdy to come outside and waited for him.

Curdy listened and said, "You're worrying about Summers being out all night?"

"He hasn't been before."

Curdy laughed. "If it'll make you happy, we can look for him."

They began at the store, and Jenkins shook his head. "He left by himself around midnight. He took all the money out of the game and broke it up. I guess he didn't see any reason to stay."

"You don't know where he went?" Curdy asked.

"Hell, I don't know. I didn't leave the store to follow him."

Outside, Curdy's face set in thought. "Maybe he found a new woman here. If so, she had to be sorry. Outside of Dawn, that's about the only kind here."

That odd feeling, Gary had known earlier, was increasing. "We'd better cover the town, Hale."

Covering the town's area didn't take much time. Summers wasn't in sight. "Gary, he's in one of these houses. Now where do we look?"

Curdy might be right, but Gary wasn't satisfied with it. "Let's go over the town again."

They passed the big tree for the second time, and Gary saw something that he had missed before. There were several brown spots in the dust, and he squatted to examine them. He poked a finger into one of them and lifted the stain for closer inspection. His eyes were narrowed as he looked up at Curdy. Curdy knew what the spots were, too; blood spots discolored by the passage of time.

Faint marks were in the dust, as though something had been dragged over it. They led to the ditch, a short distance below them. They didn't have to get clear to the ditch to see what was in it.

Both faces were set as they looked at Summers. The knife thrust had been deadly. Summers' back was covered with crusted blood, and flies buzzed over it.

"I want to talk to Munn," Curdy said in a harsh voice. "He was in that game, too."

Curdy hammered on the door of the hut that he said was Munn's. The hammering awakened Munn, for he answered it in his underwear.

Curdy hit him with it hard. "We found Summers. Knifed in the back. He's dead."

Some fleeting shock passed over Munn's face. "Do you think I have to work like that to get my money?"

Curdy's face was stubborn. "I'm not saying anything like that. But somebody knifed him. His pockets were turned out. Did he leave the game first?"

Munn squinted in thought. "He was the big winner, all right. He took all of the money out of it. But Mahoney left first. He showed hurt at his losing. Summers left next. The rest of us stayed a couple of hours later."

"Ah," Gary murmured. "You think this Mahoney was broke?"

"I know it."

Gary nodded. They had nothing yet except a pointing. "Where can we find this Mahoney?"

"If he's still in town, he'll probably be in Clayton's hut. It was empty, and Mahoney moved into it." Munn's voice sounded sincere. "Summers and I always got along all right. You call on me, if I can do anything."

Curdy bobbed his head. "We'll do that." He didn't speak again until they had turned away from the door. "What do you think, Gary?"

"I think we'd better look in on Mahoney." If Mahoney had money on him, it wouldn't be definite proof, but it would say a lot.

They paused outside the hut, and Curdy said, "If the door's unlocked, we'll go right in." He pulled his pistol. "It might be smart to be ready for anything."

He tried the door, and the latch rose. He stepped inside, and Gary was at his heels. Mahoney had been asleep, and their entrance was just pulling him out of it.

"What the hell?" His startled voice matched his face.

Curdy pointed a gun at him. "Keep your mouth shut. And don't move." He walked to the chair, beside the bed and shoved it back. A gunbelt and pistol were on top

130

of the clothes. He picked the gun out of the holster and stuck it in his waistband. "You do the looking, Gary."

Gary searched the clothes first. Nothing was in the pockets, and that neither surprised nor disappointed him. It didn't prove one thing one way, or the other. Mahoney could have buried the money someplace.

He searched the warbag next, pulling out Mahoney's things. He pulled out two items in the bottom of the bag, and his face went slack. He held a dagger gun and a watch in his hand. Those were familiar things, things Blakely always carried with him.

Mahoney's face went pinched with suspense. "I bought them from a friend," he squalled. "I don't know where he got them."

Gary moved to the side of the bed, and his eyes bored into him. "You're a liar. I think you took them off of Blakely after you killed him. That put the fear of the army in you, and you had to get from under it. You put my knife in his chest. I think you deserted because you couldn't escape the guilt."

"I didn't." Mahoney's voice rose higher. "Why do you care anyway?"

"You know. You know I was the man who was accused of it." Gary cocked the gun and thrust the muzzle into Mahoney's face. "I want the truth, or you're a dead man. Either way, I don't care much."

Mahoney must have believed that, for his eyes grew round with terror. "What good will it do you?" he whimpered. "You can't get the information back to the Army."

"I'll kill you before he has a chance," Curdy said savagely. "You waited behind that tree, then knifed Summers. You dragged him to the ditch and left him there, after you robbed him. We've got every reason to splatter your brains all over this room."

131

Mahoney tried to hold his defiance, and it collapsed all over his face.

Gary was afraid Curdy would act too quick. "Hale," he warned. "I want to take him back with me."

"He hasn't said anything yet, Gary. And I'm damned tired of waiting."

"I killed Blakely," Mahoney bleated. "I had to."

Something remote and weary was in Curdy's voice. "There it is, Gary."

Gary pondered over the loneliness in Curdy's voice, then put it aside. "I'll keep him here while you get some rope. I want him tied up every minute while I tell Dawn to get ready. And we've got to bury Summers."

He saw Curdy's face change, and he thought he understood why. "Did you think I was going to leave her here?"

"Yes," Curdy said simply. "I thought everything was changed. I'll get the rope and tell Dawn. I thought you were going to hurt her, and I couldn't stop it."

Gary thought of the loss it would bring Curdy. He could do nothing about that. "I'm sorry about her going, Hale."

"Don't you worry about that, Gary. I've known for a long time this wasn't the kind of life for her. I saw her face. She wants to go with you." Wistfulness was in his tone. "Maybe you can come back here some time."

"We can do that, Hale."

He didn't take his attention off Mahoney as Curdy went out of the door. Mahoney had done him a favor by heading here.

"Don't try to get up, Mahoney. You're alive now. You can change it."

Mahoney's eyes were big with belief.

Chapter
SEVENTEEN

Curdy finished tying Mahoney and inspected his knots. He nodded with satisfaction. "He won't go any place until we're ready for him. Dawn's getting ready. Take good care of her," he finished gruffly.

Gary nodded. He didn't have to say anything on it, but Curdy wanted the reassurance. "We're getting married in Benton, Hale."

"I figured that, Gary."

"We'd better see about getting Summers buried."

Curdy shook his head. "I looked after it. Munn and a couple of the others gave me a hand on it."

So that was what had taken Curdy so long. "I'll send that money I owe you from Benton."

Curdy grinned. "I'll worry about that." He had something on his mind that delighted him, but he had no intention of saying anything about it now.

"Munn's going with us," he said. "He's rounding up a few more. He wants to do it."

"He can't go into Benton, Hale." He didn't say it, but Curdy couldn't, either.

"He pointed out the same thing to me. He pointed out something else that's important to you. You ride into Benton, and you could be shot on sight."

Stubbornness hardened Gary's face. "I'm still going in. They'll listen to me."

"They didn't before. What if Mahoney tries to deny it to them? Which one would they believe? At the best, it would mean more court trouble. That would leave Dawn alone. At least, for a while."

"What's Munn got in his mind?"

"We'll look until we run into an Army patrol. With the number of us, they'll listen until you get it out."

It wiped Gary's stubbornness away, and he sighed in relief. "I'm grateful to you and him, too."

Curdy wiped the expression of gratitude with a gesture of his hand. "It'll break up the monotony of the days."

Eight men rode with Munn. Mahoney was roped onto his horse, and he whined about it. "I can't ride far this way."

Gary looked at him with an unfeeling eye. "Try it and see. You're better off than getting your head blown off."

They rode out of the breaks, and this was a better day than when Gary had ridden into it. But the uneasiness was still with him again. How was the army going to act until Mahoney spoke his piece? He looked over at Dawn, and she smiled at him. The radiance had been in her eyes ever since they had left. Gary told himself that everything would turn out all right; it had to.

"The breaks are behind us," Munn said flatly to Gary. "A man has to watch how he breathes. This is lawful land."

"I've got nothing against the breaks," Gary answered, and Munn grinned at him.

They rode at a slower pace, and Munn sent a man to every high elevation they reached. The man would ride up to its crest and put a pair of field glasses on the country before him. Each time he returned, he shook his head, the gesture saying he had seen nothing.

And each time, Munn would reassure Gary, "He'll see a patrol one of these times."

They were into the third day when Gary saw Pike coming down the hill at a fast speed. He was too far away to hear him, but he waved the glasses. Something had excited him.

"They're out there, Munn," Pike announced when he got close enough to talk. "I spotted them riding this direction."

"How many of them?"

"Fifteen."

Munn nodded. It wasn't too many to handle. "Could you tell which direction they're coming."

Pike grinned. "I'd say they're planning on going through Bryce canyon."

Munn returned the grin. "Then I'd say, it might be a good place for us to wait for them."

He waved his arm and put everybody into a gallop. Gary didn't know the canyon, but if it suited Munn, it was all right with him.

They rode into the canyon, dismounted, and left the horses well behind them. Munn stationed them just inside the canyon's mouth. "We've got a little wait," he said.

The men melted away into the cover of the big rocks. Gary thought it was going to be a shock for that coming patrol.

Chapter
EIGHTEEN

The waiting minutes seemed endless, and Gary fidgeted under them. It showed on his face, for Munn said, "This is a natural route for them. They'll be here."

Besides Munn, Gary couldn't see another man. They were well placed. He started to say something, and Munn held up a hand to stop. "Do I hear horses?" he asked in a low voice.

Gary listened. For a moment, there was nothing, then he caught the sound of a hoof striking a stone. It was followed by other hoof noise and the jingle of equipment chains. His throat went tight. They would be seeing the patrol in a few more minutes.

Colonel Stenton was the first rider to come into view, and Gary knew a hard satisfaction that the man led the patrol. Fourteen riders followed him, and one of them was the young sentry Gary had overcome. He hadn't permanently hurt him. That wasn't another mark the Army had on his record.

Munn waited until the patrol was strung out before them. He stood and called, "That's far enough, Colonel."

Other men rose up on both sides of the canyon, and that first sight of all those rifles must have been totally unexpected and terrifying.

Stenton sputtered and found his voice. "What's the meaning of this?"

Munn grinned at him. "We've got only eleven rifles on you, colonel. But before any of you men can pull one, we'll empty most of the saddles. Are you ready to listen?"

Stenton's eyes calculated the odds and decided that Munn was right. He gave him a sour, reluctant nod. "I know you, Munn. You don't have anything to say to me."

Munn pushed Gary forward. "No, but he has."

That was the first recognition, and Stenton's eyes flashed. "Ah, you," he said with effort.

Gary had no liking for the man. Maybe his judgment of him wasn't fair, but he couldn't help it. He pulled the dagger gun and watch from his pocket and held them forward. "Do you know these things, colonel?"

Red spots of anger showed in Stenton's cheeks, and he breathed hard. "They belonged to Captain Blakely. You were on trial for stealing them."

"Yes, but I didn't steal them. You wouldn't listen to me. I've got a deserter for you. Send him out, Munn."

Mahoney was shoved forward, his hands still tied behind his back. He stumbled and went down to his knees, and hands jerked him up again.

"Colonel, don't listen to them," Mahoney bawled. "I deserted all right, but I was ready to go back when they tied me up."

That was cunning in Mahoney's face, and Gary scowled at him. Mahoney would admit to a lesser charge and hope to get by with it.

"He killed Blakely for the gun and watch," Gary said. "He told us he stabbed him, then put my knife in the wound." He was worried as he watched the colonel. Which one was Stenton believing?

137

"Don't you believe him," Mahoney yelled. Sweat was breaking out on his forehead.

Curdy came forward and stood beside Mahoney. "He did the same thing, Colonel. After he confessed, he denied everything. This worked before. Maybe he'll change his story again."

He pulled his pistol and thrust it into Mahoney's face. "You tell the truth, or you're dead. One choice gives you a little more life. The other doesn't give you any." Curdy cocked the pistol, and its clicking was ominously loud. "You make your lie stick, and Gary doesn't have anything but to go back into the breaks. He did it before, and he can do it again."

He drew a deep breath. "All right, Mahoney."

Mahoney read the terrible intention in Curdy's face. "Don't," he bleated. The terror of staring into the yawning muzzle broke him. "I didn't mean to kill Blakely. It was an accident."

Stenton looked from Mahoney to Gary, and confused emotions struggled on his face. The embarrassed red kept burning brighter in his cheeks.

He finally managed to get it out. "I guess we were wrong."

Gary coldly stared at him. He had a lot of accusations he wanted to make, but what good would they do? "Yes," he said and wrapped it all up in the single word.

"Get Mahoney's horse," Stenton ordered his troopers. "Bind him securely on it. We'll terminate the patrol right now."

He tried to build a little favor in Gary. "We'll be happy to escort you back into Benton."

"No thanks," Gary said briefly. He started to turn away, then remembered he had some business that had to be closed with the Colonel.

"I imagine you took over my ranch and confiscated my cattle. I'll have to see you later to settle that."

The red was in Stenton's face again. "Certainly," he muttered. "We'll settle everything to your satisfaction."

He waited until Mahoney was tied in his saddle, then swept his arm forward. "Ho, forward."

Nobody said anything until the patrol was out of sight. Curdy grinned broadly. "I guess everything turned out the way you wanted it, Gary."

"Just the way I wanted it," Gary said gravely.

Those were tears in Dawn's eyes, and Gary thought Curdy's voice wasn't quite steady. He knew what Curdy felt at the parting. Didn't he feel some of the same?

Dawn hugged Curdy, and Curdy said gruffly, "You'd better be on your way."

"We'll be back one of these days," she cried. She looked at Gary, and he nodded in agreement.

Curdy reached into his pocket. He put an envelope in her hands. "I almost forgot this. Open it after we're gone."

He mounted and rode off without looking back.

Dawn fought the tears in her eyes. She looked at the envelope and tried to give it to Gary.

He shook his head. "He gave it to you."

She opened it and couldn't stop the tears as she read the short note. "This will do you two more good than it will me."

She handed the note and the money to Gary.

Gary counted it, and his face went awed. "Three thousand dollars. He can't do that."

A shaky smile was on her lips. "He wants it that way. I didn't know how much money he had saved. You take it."

Refusal was on his face before he said it. "It's yours."

139

Her smile grew. "We'll both keep it. If we don't need it, we can bring it back to him."

He wanted to hug her, but they had a long way to go, and he was impatient to get it behind them. "Let's ride."

MAVERICK GUNS BT51269 $1.25
J.E. Grinstead Western

Thunder Valley—once it had been a green, peaceful valley, but now Joe Peel, head of the ranch grabbing syndicate was causing a heap of trouble. He was looking to take Obe Carter's big cattle kingdom.

But Verne and two of his drinking buddies from the King Pin Saloon, Concho and Rile, decided to throw in their guns with the OIC bunch and fight for a seemingly lost cause.

PIÑON MESA BT51266 $1.50
Lee Floren Western

Ed Garlan had come to Piñon Mesa to raise horses south of the Border. Immediately he ran smack-dab into an outbreak of rustling which was decimating Don Alvarado's Bar S herds.

Because he was a gringo, Ed was distrusted from the outset by most of the natives of the region; when he sided with Alvarado, he also incurred the enmity of such American renegades as Sean O'Henry and Sack Colton of the Beer Bottle spread.

FAST GUN BT51227 $1.25
Walt Coburn Western

He'd killed their friend—and they were powerful. Yet they made Bryce Bradford sheriff of Buffalo Run. But then who hired the gunslingers that continued to trail him—and what did they want? The answers were hidden in his past—and Bryce had to find them before the whole town found him—dead!

THE SQUARE SHOOTER
Walt Coburn

BT51228 $1.25

Western

They called him Boone, a whipcord-tough young cowboy who drifted with a drunken outlaw named Jawbone Smith. But Boone didn't know his real name or where he came from. Only Jawbone who'd raised him knew for sure—and he had his own plans for Boone—which included turning the kid into a ruthless killer.

RIDE A CROOKED TRAIL
Burt and Budd Arthur

BT51389 $1.25

Western

It was a long and difficult trip to the Mexican border, and Ben Fleet knew that territory better than anyone. That's why the gang kidnapped him to be their guide. They'd kill him when they were safely across—unless he could escape their guns!
Setting: Southern Nevada, 1890's

THE LAWLESS ONES
Chuck Adams

BT51399 $1.25

Western

When Chet Walker came to Buckthorne it didn't take him long to realize the same people were to blame for his problems and the town's, and to get his own revenge he had to clean up the town!
Setting: Southwest U.S., 1880's

DENTON'S ARMY
Ralph Cross

BT51388 $1.75

Western

Revenge drove Bret Hastings for twenty years in search of John Denton. By the time Hastings caught up with him, Denton had a private army to back him up!
Setting: Southwest U.S., 1880's

LAST STAGE TO GOMORRAH BT51339 $1.25
Barry Cord
Western

He'd gone straight for the last few years, but Jeff Carter was still a gambler at heart, and when the man from Wells Fargo showed up, Jeff was willing to leave his ranch for the chance to find a quarter of a million dollars.

TRAIL BOSS FROM TEXAS BT51337 $1.25
Barry Cord
Western

Larry Brennan was no lawman, he was a trail boss, moving herds from one place to another. But when he got this herd to Timberlake he couldn't deliver it—the man who bought the cattle was dead! Brennan had to get involved in a range war between the ranchers and the speculators.

TRACK OF THE SNAKE BT51387 $1.75
Gene Shelton
Western

Clay Pearson raised a stake as a bounty hunter and went home to run his foster father's ranch. When he got there, the old man was dead. To claim his inheritance, Clay would have to strap on his gun again!
Setting: New Mexico, 1890's

CONVICT GUNS BT51366 $1.50
James Harvey
Western

The world changed while Dan Rogers was in prison. His girl married his worst enemy, his mother married a gambler, and no one wanted anything to do with him—except an outlaw who wanted Dan to join him. But Dan was determined to build a new life, if he had to kill to do it!
Setting: Prescott, AZ, 1870's

SEND TO: BELMONT TOWER BOOKS
P.O. Box 270
Norwalk, Connecticut 06852

Please send me the following titles:

Quantity	Book Number	Price
————	————	————
————	————	————
————	————	————
————	————	————
————	————	————

In the event we are out of stock on any of your selections, please list alternate titles below.

————	————	————
————	————	————
————	————	————
————	————	————

Postage/Handling ————

I enclose..... ————

FOR U.S. ORDERS, add 50¢ for the first book and 10¢ for each additional book to cover cost of postage and handling. Buy five or more copies and we will pay for shipping. Sorry, no C.O.D.'s.

FOR ORDERS SENT OUTSIDE THE U.S.A.
Add $1.00 for the first book and 25¢ for each additional book. PAY BY foreign draft or money order drawn on a U.S. bank, payable in U.S. ($) dollars.
☐Please send me a free catalog.

NAME ——————————————————————
(Please print)

ADDRESS ——————————————————————

CITY ———————— STATE———————— ZIP ————————
Allow Four Weeks for Delivery

144